THE CACTUS FRUITS

A JOURNEY OF AN ADIVASI LAD FROM A SERF TO THE OFFICER.

YOGESH G BHADANE

Made with ♥ on the Notion Press Platform
www.notionpress.com

Contents

Introduction

Dear Readers,

You all are reverent idol for me.

I have great pleasure in offering you this novel.

This novel is the journey of an Adivasi lad from a serf to an Officer in the Indian Army. The lad is a first-person narrator who narrates all incidents of his life without hesitation. Although he lost his all dears and nears in his life. He focused on his aim and finally, he reached his goal. The story is an inspirational journey for those who are willing to study despite all the hurdles that come in their life. It becomes a booster dose for those who believe in hard work and not in destiny. Because many people believe only in luck and destiny but this story changes their views towards life. It is a fully encouraging and optimistic story.

This novel is based on some true incidents which I collected and tried to give them my touch of imagination. The novel presents sensitive picture of the incidents the traumatic experiences of the narrator's life. Though it is entertaining and educating you. I hope you will like it. My hope is that my tastes and yours will match, at least some of the time. I shall be highly obliged, if you share your feelings about the book with me.

Thank you

Regards

Mr. Yogesh Govind Bhadane

CHAPTER ONE

Background

Kismet walks only with the hard workers, those who work hard to achieve success and believe in gaining victory over their stumbling blocks. One cannot change his kismet within a night, in a day, a month or a year. My high school teacher used to say, "If you want to change your destiny, do not give a single chance or second to gain victory over you for it. Suppress destiny with your full efforts then you can make your fortune. And only a kismet changer can give a better future to his next generation." I believed in neither kismet nor astrology but circumstances taught me to play with my destiny. Destiny and success are two sides of the page of our life. I think Success means the fulfilment of our dreams and dreams are costless or priceless, Everyone conceives dreams because to visualize dreams one should not make an effort but for the fulfillment of dreams, one has to uproot at least a thousand mountains of obstacles. I uprooted the obstacles that came in my ways of life and I am enjoying the delicious cactus fruits of common life. Today, I am celebrating the most enshrine moment of my life, the life of a father and a stage of complete maturity.

Now I realize maturity comes in humans when he becomes a father and when she becomes a mother. I am so fortunate that I can give a better future to my children. A few minutes ago, I was in a tense when my wife was on the delivery bed and struggling to give birth to my child. I prayed to God several times about the safety of my life partner and DNA. My early life was entirely different than today. It was not fully adventurous and interesting that it would inspire someone but I have to narrate it for the purgation of my soul.

I, Captain Janardan Dattu Mali, am an Officer serving in the Indian Army. I was born in a very primitive tribal community called Bhilla. Yes, Bhilla....Bhillas are the first natives of Bharata. Our ancestors were persons in the ancient history or Puranas. Generally, they lived in jungles. They were Maharshi Valmiki, Shabari Mata, Nishad Raj in Ramayana, Archer Eklavya in Mahabharata, Angulimal in the Buddhist era, Birsa Munda, Kaji Singh, Bhima Naik, Mounsi Naik, etc. During Britishraj Kaji Singh, Bheema Naik and Mousie Naik were one of the prominent rebels who revolted against the British Empire during the 1857 revolt. They were so powerful even they defeated the Britishers many times in the Gorilla War.

Our communal habitat is a replica of any slum area in a town, which is situated a half kilometre away from the main village, Deovpur. It is situated in Baglan province in the Western Ghats in Maharashtra state of India, initially known as the land of Baghs or tigers. You can find many habitats of Bhillas in various regions of Maharashtra. Deovpur is a small village having around two thousand population. It is one of the provinces of highly populated tribal communities, an ancient Aadivasi community who have been living for thousands of years of history in this area.

At the midpoint of the village, there was an ancient temple of Lord Siva. Nobody knew when it was formed but people were not interested in the temple except in the holy month of Shravan rest of the days temple became a strange thing for the villagers and the second thing it was a river that flowed only in the rainy season. One more famous temple in existence is the sacred temple of Lord Hanuman which was on the way of talk.

Our locus was well known for its scarcity of water. My grandmother told us that from the ancient era, our ancestors were living in troops in jungles later during the middle ages they were developed as Warriors or the Looteras. They were masters of runners within a second they climbed the mountains and the trees. They had physical fitness and later they were involved in burgling to loot various money lenders as well as rich persons but they didn't loot middle-class or poor people.

We didn't find the historical monuments of our community because we had been living in the jungles since the primitive era and our forefathers never developed writing skills or writing literature to write their events for the upcoming generations and from the ancient era, Pen was the instrument which was used in the hands of only some selected people that's why the history of the book was written on only the lives of kings, aristocratic, Brahmins and priests not on the biographies of poor working strata and Adivasis.

Bhillas were living in jungles and the whole land of that area belonged to the community. Every generation has been adopting the changes according to the time and become the part of at least a developing society but my community is deeply rooted in one place. We have a long history but my ancestors were not interested in education that's why before my two generations they worked as slaves on the farms and they lost their ownership, they lost their lands and became serfs. My habitat locale was panoramic and rich with natural resources. That was especially known with the various species of squirrels and birds like little sparrows, Maiyna, Parrots, Doves, Lawari, Titur, Cuckoo, Hummingbirds, Shimpi, Crows, Cranes etc. The people from my shoal came together on weekly market day in the morning and hunted squirrels and shooted Titurs with Gullars. They are usually interested in hunting animals like deer, wild cats, rabbits and all kinds of birds except crows because it was considered a bad omen. They were all masters in shooting with Gullars. It is made from dual branches of trees and a rubber tube to hit stones on the pray. The market day was on Saturday so, from Sunday to Friday they went to work as banduwa majdoors under the clutches of landlords or any rich farmer. Their masters paid them a few rupees at the weekend for their survival. They all were banduwa majdoors because they borrowed money from the farmers for various reasons like marriage festivals, birthdays, funerals, and hospital expenditures etc. Mostly, all were illiterate because from childhood their parents sent them to work on the farms to decrease the burden of their debts instead of school.

And we were not alone on this earth to work under the clutches of a particular community's. Our all relatives were working in somebody's farmhouse, in somebody's poultry farm, in somebody's onion storehouses, in somebody's Garden as Gopher. The farmers took the benefits of their illiteracy and engaged their heirs in the fields. The cycle of debts could not be cracked by my people because they hated strict school masters and the school expenses as well as the school distance.

The farmers from our region reaped pomegranates, grapes, sugarcanes, tomatoes and other vegetables etc. Our region received healthy monsoon and it had many water bodies, the lands were fertile and produced a quality of crops in a big quantity but the environment had been changed after deforestation and involvements of fertilizers. But my grandmother claimed that nature changed because people's purity changed.

I don't know the exact date of my birth but I know, I was born in the hands of my grandmother. I had two elder siblings Chanda and Soni. My mother's name was Sandhya, a symbolic name that means evening and as per her name, she only faced evenings of life not any good mornings of life. She was not so much fair but had a charming and glowing face. She did not use any make-up in her entire life. My father forced her to use at least Ponds talcum powder in the evening on her face. She was a very patient and hard-working lady. My grandmother's name was Sarla. She used to chew tobacco and eat mutton of He-goat at the weekend. She was a well-known brawler lady, She had a deep knowledge of Junglee animals, weeds and Ayurvedic plants. She never looked like an old lady because she was fourteen years older than my father. She behaved manfully in our community. She didn't like to go and work on farms and some ladies from our neighbourhood said to my mother, that every three days in the afternoon, Sarla went to the outer part of the village where some Muslim people were living and met a Muslim Mulla. But my mother who was exactly opposite nature of my grandmother, did not entertain them and remained silent. She never took interest in the rumours as well as other gossip of ladies. Even she never tried to talk with the neighbours. She just engaged herself with her daughters.

Generally, our people are not interested in God but she was a devotee of Lord Krishna and named me Janardan, one of the names of Lord Shri Krishna. My grandfather, who was already dead before my birth so, I did not know about him, but my grandmother lived him in her stories sometimes. Dattu, my father, my first and last hero in life, was a lion-hearted person but a drunkard sometimes like other people in our community. He followed the path of my grandfather because my grandfather died when my father was young and he died because he was an inveterate man of alcohol called Daru. Daru is made from various flowers collected from jungles. It has a special name Moha Daru and it was available at a very cheap rate but once someone becomes addicted to drinking that beverage, it will never leave anyone in life till the end. My father was slim and physically sturdy. He had a black hippy hairstyle, black eyes, brown face but handsome man. He was a mad fan of Bollywood actor Mithun Chakravarthy, he watched Mithun Da's film 'Yugandhar' several times, and even he claimed that Mithun Da belonged to our community and was his blood relative. He usually compared Mithun Da's filmy life with the life of serfs. He was only Fifth class passed person but he had a strong aspiration that his son would become a Primary teacher. Unfortunately, I was unable to fulfil my father's dream to become a Primary teacher but he would be satisfied in heaven that his son successfully cracked the chain of heritage. The chain of hereditaments which I got from my father and my grandfather.

My father was a bondsman who was working under the control of a landholder called Balasaheb Patil, an orthodox Maratha farmer. My father didn't remember when he started his work or career as a serf on the farm. My father and my grandfather worked as helots on Bala Patil's farm. My father used to say to me when he was in a drunken situation that his great-grandfather was one of the warriors in Kaji Singh's Platoon who was a rebel during the British era in the Khandesh region of Maharashtra state in India. He continued "He was the greatest warrior and he looted many Savkars or money lenders, landlords, liegemen, during that era and distributed the whole wealth among tribal people but he never hid a single gold ring for his family, such a generous person he was ! he left just ten-acre fertile land as an estate for his next generations. But my father sold that land in a drunken mood for only just a hundred rupees to Balasaheb Patil's father Ganapatrao. He fought later to regain it in the court but his all efforts failed because Patils had a political background and according to the Indian court laws, Ganapatrao purchased the land on a ninety-nine-year bond. My father had lost everything. He became an inebriated person and debtor. He searched for work and money to give fees of lawyers and livelihood but nobody would give him anything. Finally, he took debt from boorish Ganapatrao for livelihood and mortgaged freedom. Later we know, that Ganapatrao threatened everyone not to help my father. What a destiny stroke that he was working as a serf on his land. My grandfather was a warrior who fought against the powerful Britishraj. My father lost our ten-acre land in an alcoholic mood and I remain the main serf of their family and it will continue generation to generation." This background history was revealed by him.

Seventy families were living in my confraternity. It had been maintaining some rituals since the primitive era. There was a ritual in our community that if a child was born in someone's family or newly bride or bridegroom before and after marriage, the head of the family immediately arranged a function. For it the head need not need to invited someone, just passed the oral message and all community and all families would remain present up to the evening of the day. They directly resumed any urgent work to attend the function. Suppose, someone did not receive the message, that person would directly blame the head and without arguing involved and enjoy the function. The function contrived for the next three days, it started with offering Daru to everyone. All men and some women enjoyed the beverage except children. Later, dal rice and Bundi means sweet made from maida and sugar prepared for lunch and dinner. The same function was arranged when someone passes away. This was a unique feature of my community.

My father had taken a thousand rupees as a loan from his master Bala Patil and for the celebration of my birthday, that means I was born with a loan. That day was a memorable day for my parents because they were giving a grand feast for our community. So, usually, Mama and Father were extremely happy, the state of happiness was related to benefaction and satisfaction to humans. My father had arranged a function on the encounter with my birth. My Mama, maternal uncle, living in a tribal village who was a manufacturer of Moha Daru arranged four big containers on the occasion. The function continued to the next three days.

I was the third child of my mother. When I was born, she was so happy maybe that was the first moment of happiness she met in her life. My mother was a very hard worker lady, she went to work on the farm of a farmer and tied me on her shoulder or her back with Fadaki, a low-quality blanket. Whenever a farmer or landlord came to call my whole family to work on wages, my father Appa forced my siblings to go with my mother to work. My grandmother and mother usually argued with Appa and defended our sides when he forced my two elder sisters to work on the farm despite they were only four and six years old. Because somehow he became restless when he failed to earn money for our bread and butter. Later, he repented on his actions but he knew that he could not change the malicious fortune of his family and the chain of slaves.

Bala Patil is one of the rude characters of my journey of life. As everybody met a villainous character in his life like that he was one of the people who steered my life. Balasaheb Patil had a round face with wound marks on it a big talwar-sized moustache and a curved bear, his colour was black. He was around six feet and roaring voice. His eyes were very dark with red colour. He was educated but not literate in his attire like any other landowner of Devpur.

Bala Patil was a loutish person his forefathers cheated my great-grandfather and grabbed our land. Like ourselves, my confraternity lost their lands under other farmers' clutches. He had seventy acres of fertile land with various sources of water. He belonged to one of the wide classes of Maharashtra i.e. Kunabi. Kunabi's claimed that they were Marathas. The word means henchmen of sacred land. They were worshippers of Panduranga an avatar of Lord Shri Krishna and warriers of Chhatrapati Shivaj Maharaj. So, they all proudly called themselves Kunbis. Their population was wide. But unfortunately, some of them became wolfish and lost their chastity due to addiction to alcohol and town signoras and they threatened and suppressed other strata according to their intentions. My grandmother hated them from the bottom of her heart. So, She never went to work in any farmer's land.

On the third day, after the occasion Bala Patil came to our juggi and called father means Appa. He roared, Are you celebrating the occasion throughout the year? Abe bhenchod four days are already over, I am facing loss at my farm, you are responsible for my loss and you have to recover it, you won't get a single day of leave for the next four years, send your two daughters for plucking tomatoes and uprooting onions and I don't want to listen 'No', Don't forget you have borrowed 70000 rupees on your father death. I don't know how you can pay my debts, I think, it will carry up to your children. if your daughters started to work in my farm, still at the age of twenty five you will at least repay my half of the loan."

Appa mumbled, "But Aba, I got a son, he told him in enthusiasm, you should bless him, I will train him to learn, he will become a teacher and I will repay everything to you".

"Are a drunkard person, your level is a level of serf, Remember my words he will not gain interest in education, Don't waste your efforts, he will roam everywhere to hunt birds within five years. Don't see dreams with your open eyes these kinds of dreams will not be fulfilled. Remember you are an Adivasi, you all are born to work only on farms. You people don't have your brains. I don't want to waste my words, don't waste your time and come within half an hour and start working. I am going to market and will return in the evening, before my return, you must pluck all the tomatoes and pomegranates. I don't want to listen to any excuses. He smiled cunningly and turned back his bullet towards the market road. He moved his bullet spreading smoke on Appa's face.

My grandmother was peeping from the door towards Appa and Bala Patil. She came near Appa and roared, "I better know him, he is a bastard not only he but his whole community is bastard they are never trying to rescue us from their clutches even you worked up to hundred years and whenever you will sit it take the whole hisab that time they would show you lakhs rupees as loan and burden. This is a curse for us and I pray that you don't involve our children in this hierarchy. Please have to understand and search the another way. You are drinking

Daru and wasting money and how could we repay his whole debt? You should do something to free them from their clutches. At least, my last desire is, that my next generation must not dip into the mortgage of Bala Patil." My Grandmother relieved her stress.

My mother secretly listened to the dialogue and interrupted, "Can we search another way of livelihood?"

"You idiot you couldn't understand anything, Before it you were just born here to produce children and to work like a bull on a farm. You do not have any knowledge of life. I am fifth standard passed but you are a completely illiterate woman you don't know anything about his hisab. If our children are not working in their farms at least they would rescue our children from their clutches up to the end of their life. If our children start to work from this moment they will reduce complete loan up to half of the age. So, we would not do anything new. Now, I am going, he is waiting for me. Otherwise, he will shout at me", Appa relieved his stress on my mother.

"Don't you want to carry your meal", Mother shouted.

"No, It's OK and I don't want to waste my time. My Malkin is a generous lady and will give me enough food. She will give me two bhakaries and a piece of pickle in the afternoon ", he responded.

"Ho! She will give you the stale food which they are going to throw anywhere", she ridiculed.

"Arre they are giving us food, for our stomach and cloth for our body. They do some generous act, Why are you cursing these people? Now, I don't want to argue with you, go ahead." Appa ran hurriedly towards Bala Patil's farm.

He reached the farm at morning 8 o'clock, suddenly a roaring voice came into his ears, you came again late haramkhor. You will go at 9 p.m. You rascal fed cattle and go to fetching water to tomatoes, onions. Appa ironically smiled, "Balaji I will finish the work as soon as."

Suddenly, a melodic voice of Kalpana came into his ear, "Dattu take a tea".

She called him from the backyard. Appa went there, and urged to Vahinisaheb in a low voice, " Is night food remaining ?" I am so much hungry, If you have something to eat, give me I will eat in the afternoon."

"Speak slowly, come after an hour when your Malik will go to the Bazaar and my Sasubai would busy in enchanting. I will give you like every day's routine." She spoke softly.

CHAPTER TWO

A Cage Bird

Kalpana was a beautiful and innocent lady. She was the third wife of Bala Patil. My father used to say that Bala Patil and his mother killed and burned his first wife and pushed his second wife into the well because their parents refused to give him gold chains and necklaces. The police sided Bala because he was the brother-in-law of an MLA. So, nobody dared to complain about Bala. Kalpana was fifteen years younger than him and she was the daughter of his mother's distant brother. She didn't cross the boundary of the bungalow.

The roaring voice of Bala appeared , "Dattya have you done the work, Now come here and prepare spray for grapes and listen you didn't bring your daughter today, but tomorrow you have to come with your daughter because we have to pluck tomatoes. I don't want to listen to anything telling them he kicked his bullet and went toward the marketplace as he did every day's routine.

Appa uprooted weeds, cut the grass for cattle, fed cattle, and sprayed for the grapes. Appa worked with an empty stomach. He came to feed for cattle in the shade which was situated in the backyard of the Bungalow. He was talking with the cows, "You are so lucky that you are getting food without struggling but I have to pay freedom for food. There is no difference between you and me only the difference is between I am a man and you are an animal." The cattle shook their heads. Suddenly, he heard the whisper of Kalpna. She gestured to him and called him to the backyard. Appa was removing the sweat and breathing fast.

She called him in low voice, "Dattu come here and drink some water".

She very much knew that if she called him for lunch her mother-in-law, Yashoda would scold him. Yashoda was keenly observing her daughter-in-law. She was an Orthodox. So, Kalpana called Appa to drink water secretly, rolled three stale chapatis with pickles and handed them over to him with kind gestures. The characters of Kalpana and Yashoda were quite controversial. Yashoda was a malicious and conservative lady, she never showed any mercy on poor strata people.

After the sunset, he had over almost his work and he wanted to return home to play with me. Because I was only a male child in his life. He wanted to see or enjoy his childhood in the form of me. He loved my two elder sisters but he was very much afraid of the society about daughters. Appa returned home late in the night.

Generally, Appa did not allow my mother to go and work on the farm until my birth. Despite service, his thinking was different than any other person's. His philosophy was different. He wanted to educate us because he knew the importance of education as per Doctor Ambedkar. He said, 'Education is tigress milk those who drink he will roar.' He never read any book but he wanted his daughters and son must take higher education at least a school education. His dream was his son would become a primary teacher and his daughters would get married to e-government employees. And Iam his son believed that Destiny made many obstacles and barriers in our way only those who try to break the mountains and barriers, can get success. Only a few people can do this. But whenever they walked on that path thousands of times they lost their hopes and tried to stop fighting with destiny but fortunately, I was not that kind of person I fought with destiny continuously and one day destiny except my strength and today I am a captain in Indian Army.

But this was not in my people's fate because our people were denied education. They cannot leave for more than five days without working. The reason is that they do not have their property, they do not have their lands, pakka houses and no fixed income sources. So, the day that go to work they would get bread on the same day. Apart from that, their shoulders were fully loaded with the loans that defaulted loans which were forcefully given by landlords.

The next day, Appa hurriedly went to the farm of Bala Patil with an empty stomach. My grandmother came out of Juggi and called Appa to come back to take lunch from a distance. Appa reached the farm. Firstly, he collected cow dung and threw it in a garbage area, cut a heap of grass and fed the cattle. There were hot summer days and for some relief, he sat in a cowshed.

Appa muttered," Oh! God what kind of life you have given me even if I could not enjoy some moments of happiness with my family, please show me another way."

The wife of Bala Patil, Kalpana was a very kind lady. She had already a five-year-old daughter. Her mother in law always expecting a son from her. She had a soft corner toward my father.

In the afternoon she came into the backyard looked at my father affectionally and said "How is your child, Dattu? I think you are quite satisfied because you became a father of a son and how unfortunate am I ! that I could not give a son as an heir to my family. Kalpana spoke in a discouraged voice. "

"But vahini saheb you are a mother of a daughter and Bhagwan cannot discourage a fair lady like you." Appa boosted her courage.

'Yes but it's not a complete truth, you know inner satisfaction is very important in a woman's life. When I got married I came to this house with various dreams but right now I remained only as a scarecrow", A bird in a golden cage without hopes of freely flying in the open sky", Kalpana spoke in a disappointed tone.

" But Vahini saheb Aba loves you so much and you are very fortunate that you are living in a palace with all amenities. People like us just think and we cannot see a dream of this kind of amenities." Appa spoke.

" This is an only illusion because a lady cannot live with a drunken person if she knew before the marriage about somebody's addiction. A lady cannot get ready to marry such a person. " She answered.

"Means you are not happy with..... ." Appa astonished.

She looked towards Appa with hopeful eyes, "A married woman cannot use insulting words with her husband, she bears everything in her life for the sake of her husband. Even we ladies pray to banyan tree about the same person as a husband in the next life but sometimes my mind is not ready to do it." Kalpana spoke in a low voice.

"Don't worry Vahini Sahib God is graceful, he will bless you with a son". Appa encouraged her.

Kalpana didn't say or react, she moved into the house. She was pregnant for three months. Every dawn she sat in front of Devgrah to pray God for a son.

Days passed rapidly. Kalpana was suffering from peripartum in the nine month. She yelled, Oh! God leave me, free me from the terrible pain. Atyaji do something".

"Wait it is your exam' Hey Bhagwan! bless us with a male child, I want an heir for my family", Yashoda encouraged her.

I am calling Dattu, "Dattu, where are you? come here. Yashoda roared. Appa reacted and came.

"Where is Bala?", She asked.

"I don't know, maybe he went to taluka" Appa answered innocently.

"Do ready our ambassador, Dattu, we have to move to the hospital," Yashoda ordered.

"But Akka Saheb our van has some problems. I think we have to take help from our neighbour Mali Kaka in this urgency." Appa said instantly.

"He is our rival how can he help us? We must check other options." Yashoda mumbled.

"Don't worry I am doing something". Appa ran towards Mali Kaka's farm and came in a few minutes with a Mini tractor. Mali Kaka understood the situation and gave his tractor.

Appa called Yashoda, "Here is a tractor".

Yashoda ordered him, "Call somebody to lift her",

"But nobody is here, now", Appa replied.

"Lift her and take her into the tractor trolley", Yashoda said angrily.

Appa hesitately came near Kalpana and lifted her with full force. She held his neck tightly and stopped her yelling for a moment. She was pretty shy in his arms at the moment. Appa carried her into the hospital with Yashoda. Doctors took her into the ICU ward. After half an hour, she gave birth to a beautiful girl child. The doctor came out of the ICU and called Appa, "Congrats her delivery was normal and she is safe now, she gave birth to a girl child".

Yashoda interrupted, "How is baby? I think doctor, you have to recheck baby. She has given birth to a baby boy."

"I am not wrong Aunty, she gave birth to a Lakshmi, a girl. You all are fortunate, delivery is normal and the baby is fair and healthy", the Doctor replied with enthusiasm.

" What a baby girl! Have you checked the doctor? You can't say this because I sent her a few months before to her father's home to check the baby's status, which means her father deceived me, Madarchod person!", Yashoda cried.

"Enough and old lady to check baby status during pregnancy is a crime. I can complain about you", the doctor vociferated.

Yashoda sat stunningly at the corner of the hospital. Kalpana's parents came in the middle of the day. Suddenly Appa bought Jilebi and offered to Yashoda. Yashoda refused to take it. Appa turned towards Kalpana's father, "Patil Dada this is a good omen, we have to enjoy it".

" You are right, I have daughters when they were born I gave grand feasts and disbursed sarees among my countrymen."

While replying, Annasaheb turned towards Yashoda with a piece of jilebi. "Take it Vahinbai and remember if you pinch out continuously my daughter, I warn you, many incidents occurred frequently about accidents of mother-in-laws in our society." The cold sweet came out of Yashoda's face.

Annasaheb called Appa, "Dattu you are a perfect human being, take a hundred rupees and purchase mithai for all." Annasaheb gave two hundred rupees to Appa and said, "The remaining amount is yours as a prize from us." A real Lakshmi blessed Appa on that day. Appa bought groceries and mithai for us. But Bala Patil never visited the hospital. He drank much more on that day in misery. Because he had already received the news in the evening.

Appa returned home in the evening and bought chicken. We celebrated the birth of a baby girl at our home. My mother and sisters praised the birth of Bala Patil's daughter birth.

The next day, Appa went to his regular work, Appa found Bala Patil in a sleepy mood on the veranda. Appa tried to awake but Bala drank out of the limit before sleeping. So Appa took him into the bedroom. Kalpana was admitted four days in a hospital but Bala Patil never went there. Surprisingly, Yashoda stayed at the hospital to take care of her daughter-in-law. She ordered Appa to come regularly to the hospital, even though she bought dried dates, coconuts, laddus and apples for her daughter-in-law. Every morning and evening Appa went to the hospital and affectionally asked Kalpana's health.

He surprisingly asked Yashoda, How she had changed her behaviour towards Kalpana Vahini. She smiled and answered, "I was in the same state as Kalpana, the world is round, Dattu. Sometimes we have to change ourselves according to the current days "

On the last day, Yashoda hired an auto for her daughter-in-law. She warmly welcomed Kalpana in her bungalow. Even she gave five hundred rupees to Appa as a Bakshis. She said to Appa, "Purchase new clothes for your entire family and take two days' leave, This Saturday enjoy with your family in the weekly market."

Appa's Joy did not have a limit and he concluded that it happened because of my birth. He was assured that I would change his destiny and break the entire chain of poverty. In the evening he went to the temple of lord Hanuman and offered roses to Him.

If a person is a drunkard and lusty his thinking capacity becomes rotten he can't think of his family's welfare in that mood. Bala Patil came home late in the night to home and entered his room. He entered the room in a cruddy mood. Kalpana was Feeding her baby on the bed. He rushed into the bedroom lifted the baby and took her into the Palna. He vehemently pulled her and started to suck the breast of her. She yowled painfully and tried to oppose him.

Suddenly, Yashoda entered the room with a big bamboo and blew him, "I know you swine, rowdy, directly entered the bedroom. You must be ashamed of your behaviour. Don't you understand the condition of a recently pregnant lady? You never thought about her before. Get lost, a boar and not to enter the room without my permission. You Kasai, even though I never tried to enter your room before, I knew your mentality, that's why I was awake just leave the room now." Bala muttered and left the room. Yashoda heard the throbbing voice of a bullet.

The next morning, Yashoda called Kalpana's father to take her home. Yashoda goodbye to her with five kilos of laddu, dried fruits, apples, almonds and Kaju. Yashoda advised her father not to send her for at least the next four months. Her father Annasaheb came to receive her. He wanted to ask something Yashoda but before asking Kalpana shook her eyes at her father. Annasaheb understood everything and so he did not say anything. Appa loaded Kalpana's luggage in Annasaheb's van. Annasaheb's van disappeared leaving smoke behind.

CHAPTER THREE

A Fair of Joy

The next day, was Saturday a day of the weekly Bazaar and that Saturday was the season of fair. So, it was a fair Saturday. The fair was held on the occasion of the local deity Mhasoba and we believed that he was an avatar of lord Shiva. The fair was held at Taluka Place. Appa woke up very early in the morning, he awoke all of us even my grandma with him. He ordered us to keep ready as soon as possible. I was around a year old so, I did not much understand the joy of fair but my elder sisters and mother were extremely happy. They didn't want to lose a single moment of enjoyment at the fair. After all the fair brings balloons and happiness to working-class people in the countryside.

After the bath, my grandmother applied her favourite pond powder on her face. My mother made six bhakri's with green chilli chutney. We started our journey towards Taluka. It was twelve km away from our Basti. Appa lifted my younger sister on his shoulder. My mother lifted me in her lap and my elder sister was with my grandmother. The journey began with singing folk songs and whistling. My Appa was filmi shouking and adopted the style of Mithun Da. The songs of Mithun Dada's Disco Dancer, Pyaar Jukata Nahi and many more movies. My innocent mother gave chores behind his songs and my grandmother shook her head with gutka in her mouth. We reached the mid-day in the fair. The fair was a grand festival.

People from three talukas and thirty-five villages came to enjoy the grand fair. Appa first took all of us to the temple of Mhasoba. He purchased a coconut and Peda. He broke the coconut in front of Mhasoba and offered a small plumy piece and peda, which the rest of the Prasad distributed among us. My elder sister took a huge share amongst us, she liked wet coconut and it was the most delicious food that she received after a long time. My younger sister gobbled up three Pedhas in a morsel. They behaved like they won the lottery. We started moving into the fair. Slowly, we enjoyed watching the stalls of toys, garments, shoes, chappals, ladies' imitation jewellery, shawls, blankets, bed sheets, pillows etc. The separate lanes and Gallies had arranged various items. The first Galli was the Galli of utensils of steel and plastic items. Next was chappal Galli, which was followed by wooden household objects, Behind it there was a Galli of decorative items, plastic toys, various sarees, clothes, readymade dresses, Steel kothis i.e. trunks etc. My mother bought a new belan, poli pat and paraat. She was happy that my Appa first time bought her a new design chappal. He gave plastic chappals to our siblings. My grandmother took her thaili (cotton pouch) and bought ponds talcum powder, jhumkas, and Painjans. She bought a pair of Painjans and a frock for my elder sister Chanda. Later, we moved towards watching the Mout ka Kuwah show. My mother and sisters were afraid of watching the stunts of bike riders. My mother could not believe such scenes of motorbikers.

Then Appa took us to the most famous show of Pannalal Gadha show. Primarily, my mother and grandmother opposed Appa going there, but Appa took all of us forcefully into the show. The show was amazing and a prime attraction of the fair. Pannalal was an ass.

The announcer asked Pannalal, "Pannalal go and find out who comes here as a loafer?" Pannalal hurriedly went and stood near a young man with a hippy haircut". The Crowd burst into laughing. "Achcha Pannalal finds out an innocent lady in our show. Then he came and stopped near my mother. The whole audience was impressed. The announcer appealed to Pannalal, "Now find out the Romeo in our crowd?" Pannalal went and stood near a college-going boy who was continuously adjusting his hairstyle. The whole audience was showering with laughing. Pannalal found the beauty queen as a beautiful girl who was standing at the last corner of the show.

Finally, the announcer appealed, " Pannalal, please show us the heroine figure amongst us who will receive a ten rupees note". Pannalal came near my father and held his shirt in his mouth. My Appa won ten rupees note in the show. Appa was the first time honoured with a prize in his lifetime. He accepted that note as he had received the world's most prestigious award. In that state of happiness, Appa took all of us in Photoshop and took a family photo. Appa holds that 10 rupees prize in his right hand. He set the note as came in the photo. That was a glorious moment for my family. Then we sat in a giant Wheel chart and rode on a giant boat. In the evening,

Appa took all of us to eat Pav-wada, Bhatta, Jilebi and Guddi Shev.

He packed a kilo of Jilebi for our home. Appa spent at least three hundred rupees. He bought new clothes for all of us and a big toy truck of wooden for me. Then the day became dark, and my mother suggested, " We would reach at midnight, it would be better to stay at my distant brother's home".

"But his home is not enough for all of us. He has only a room. So we must have to move our home ", Appa uttered.

Appa first time hired an auto with fifty rupees which was very costly for us. We returned to our home. We all were happy and dipped into the pleasure. My sister continuously watched their new clothes and they slept while taking their belongings in their laps. That was the collective happiness of my family. After all, it is true that money puts smiles and happiness on our faces. We can purchase happiness with money.

I also slept with hugging the wooden truck. The next morning, Appa wore the old tattered shirt. Suddenly my grandmother roared, "You can wear good clothes now".

"No, I am not a government servant, I am a serf and I have to work in a farm with pesticides. I am keeping all those new clothes for the functions or any good occasion." Appa answered and turned back. My mother handed over two Bhakari and pickles rolled out in a white cloth as his meal.

CHAPTER FOUR

The Cactus Fruits

Soon days passed rapidly, I became five years old in the summer. So, my Appa decided to write my name in a school. Fortunately, three teachers, two ladies and a sir came to our Basti, confraternity to seek school admissions, they were from an Adivasi boarding school. They visited every Juggi and enquired about new enrollments. They met Appa and convinced him to send me and my sister except elder into the school. Firstly, my grandmother and mother were not ready to send us but my Appa knew the importance of education. He persuaded them and told the teachers to come to pick us up the next week. That day the teachers earned at least twenty-five admissions from our confraternity.

The teachers got a big treasure that year. My elder sister did not fit in their criteria because she was more than thirteen years old. My Grandmother asserted, "We can't send our girls far away from our homes after the age of twelve & that boarding school is thirty km away from us. I heard the teachers from the school send all boys & girls to their farmyard for work instead of teaching, all the girls are busy cooking & washing the clothes of residential teachers. Sorry, I wouldn't allow my granddaughter to go there."

My elder sister was the reflection of my grandmother & my grandmother looked like herself in her attire. She could not live without my elder sister. Finally, the day came, The teacher came to our Basti with hired a 407 mini truck to carry us. I stuck to my mother like a lizard, and my sister disappeared. Appa held my hand & lifted me in the van. Appa knew us so he went into our backyard & picked out the Bamboo basket of hens. There he caught my sister Soni. Appa lifted her & pushed her into the van trolly. My mother gave us a big bag of nylon, she kept dried berries in that bag. Parents handed over their children to the teachers. Our horde was ready to send children to school due to my Appa's decision. They all imitated Appa. All the children started yelling & parents reacted the same as they saw their hearts were crying. The whole Basti was covered with only yelling & crying. Even the passerby thought that some terrible mishap would be happened there. Appa was almost in the mood to cry but he didn't show any emotions on his face. Because that was the first step towards the dream of my Appa. We reached the school in the afternoon, a peon carried our luggage and two lady teachers welcomed us with Aarti. Some of us did not come out from trolly. But at the gate, the principal lady distributed pedha and barfi to everybody. I held my sister's hand and took Pedha & returned to the van. Maybe we thought the van again carried us to our homes.

The principal came near us & said, "Welcome all my dear friends, we are watching a movie together then a cartoon or a puppet show in our language. We will not touch to the book, we will play various games every day, after two weeks we will go for trekking & excursion. I promise we will take all of you into the fair to take a ride on giant wheels & moving wooden horse chart. Every Saturday & Sunday you will get Jilebi & Bundi laddoos. Even today the feast is ready with jilebi.

We all looked at each other The principal showed us the dining hall, and The smell of tasty Jilebi and masala Khichdi reached us. That increased our hunger. Me and Soni Tai decided to march towards lunch. My Appa persuaded me to take an interest in the study. That's why he told me stories of national leaders, struggling actors, and historical kings every night before sleeping. At first sight, The school looked like a jail for us. A huge fence was built around the school, it had only a gate so nobody could run from the school. The feast was amazing & delicious but that feast was not for the old students. The old students served us in thali & gave us water in a glass after lunch. The principal ordered us to sit as it was.

She addressed, "Now this thali & glass is yours, they belong to you every day at a time of supper, lunch & breakfast you should carry these utensil & immediately wash after use. Every morning you will get a boiled egg & biscuits, Khichdi or dal rice for lunch, tea & toast in the evening & two sabji's, rotis & rice for dinner. Now, you will go to your room, our warden teacher will show you, your rooms. Boys will go to Block no 1. and girls will go to Block No. 2. No boy will go to the girl's block & no girl will go to the boys' block even brothers & sisters are not allowed to go to each other rooms. We all are family, here all are our brothers & sisters, in case you face any difficulty. You can come to meet me, one more thing, you will receive everything in your room a bed, blanket, pillow, towel, soap, oil, powder, uniform, shoes etc. Your roommate is your buddy. You can't go elsewhere without your roommate. He or she is your brother & sister. Now go with your warden teacher."

Soni Tai was crying after leaving me. She received her roommate from Ambewadi & surprisingly her roommate Mangal Tai's younger brother became my roommate, Narayan. My first & lifetime friend Narayan. It was 15th June, the first day of school. But we never touched any educational object on that day. The principal instructed all staff not to disburse books or stationery at least for the next five days among students. Her aim was clear, She wanted to root all of us in the school, so she allowed her staff to play with all of us. Teachers played cricket, hide & seek, chasing, Goli, langdi etc with us. Temporarily, we forgot our family bonding.

The next day, the warden woke us in the morning for bathing. I did not understand why most of the students were scared of bathing. The warden forcefully dragged the scared children to the bathroom and started showering Students came out of the bathroom yelling & crying. First five days teachers did not give stationery. We spent a few days trying to understand each other and adjust ourselves to the environment. We were six students in the room but Narayan became my shareholder. We did not leave each other. We bath together, eat together, play together, study together and sleep together.

We received books and other stationery with a khaki bag on the sixth day. I was curious about learning but Narayan did not have an interest in studying. His interest was in Nature, he was a lover of nature from childhood. First five days, We learned alphabets, numbers, & stories. Then Sunday came, and teachers allowed us to go outside the school Fench but we were under the surveillance of wardens. There, we ran behind butterflies, plucked wild flowers, made Basuri from Bamboo even Naru made Pipani from Awali's branches. But he had skill in playing Gullar to shoot birds. He kept a small Gullar in his pocket and shot two hummingbirds in two shots. I stopped him & asked why he shot the birds.

He answered, "We roasted the birds on fire after hunting, Their meat is so tasty and you cannot compare their meat with any animal's meat, If we get a chance to do it, I will roast a bird for you". Then he pulled me near a cactus tree, he showed me cactus fruits, that cactus fruits fully covered with sharpened thorns. "Janya this is my favourite fruit, I am dam sure that you haven't tasted it before," Naru concluded.

" No, I don't know about it what's that? I hadn't tasted it before what's its name?, Tell me", I curiously inquired.

“These are fruits of Cactus, It appeared after seven years on its tree, it's fully covered with poisonous thorns but its fruits are rich with all medicinal properties, juicy and luscious. It's red and pink colour attract the bees but it is not easy to pluck the fruits. My grandmother said that it's very much useful for sweet blood patients, It was gifted by Lord Hanuman to us. But I don't understand what is sweet blood patient. Do you Know? He continuously talked and asked.

"Sorry," I answered.

He took a stick and hit the fruits. The fruits dashed on the ground. Naru didn't touch the fruits directly, he carefully removed thorns with a stick and gave pinky luscious wild cactus fruits. The fruits were so tasty and became my favourite. I never forget such kind of mouth savouring taste. The fruits became my favourite and were gifted by Lord Hanuman. I concluded after tasting.

Suddenly, the whistle blew & we left our prayer there. Narayan was upset to enter the premises of the school. From the next morning, the daily schedule began and we engaged in our daily routine. But Narayan was eagerly waiting for the Sunday.

CHAPTER FIVE

The Storm

From the next morning, the daily schedule began and we engaged in our daily routine. But Narayan was eagerly waiting for the Sunday. Five months passed rapidly. The the season of Diwali came, our exam was over. The mini truck 407 picked up and left us at our homes. Now, we felt like strangers at our homes. Because the school changed our mentality, it taught us common courtesy, and how to behave. How to do our work.

Firstly, I hugged my mother, she was so shocked to see us because they did not have any idea about our coming or news. My elder sister looked at us kneely and slightly jealous of us. In the evening Appa came home. When he saw us, he was so happy to meet me, he hugged me tidily and kissed on my forehead. "How is your study? What did you learn in your school? How are your teachers? Where they were given food on time or not? Have they sent you to work on a farm? You looked so thin, I think you are working hard on the farm instead of studying. Tell me everything, I won't send you again in that school again. I will write your name in our ZP School",Appa talked continuously.

"Appa, now I am grown up. The teachers are so friendly and never told us any personal work. They did not send us to the farmyard. We got the best khichdi, eggs, tea, Jilebi,dal-rice, roti &sabji on time. Even Look at my uniform, and shoes, we get everything. Our teachers are more than our family. I learnt 1 to 100 numbers in three months. I can read & write my full name. I can show you", I deliberately answered my Appa's curiosity.

" You are my dream, son, I wouldn't let you work like me, you must break the chain of our heritage, you must make a new world for yourself, don't worry about us but you must fly in the unlimited sky for it you have only one option and that is education, you must have to pass Higher Secondary School. You should become a primary teacher and help our community children to educate", Appa carefully explained.

"I will become a teacher ", I satisfied him.

Appa's daily routine has not changed yet. He woke up early, got ready and marched towards Bala Patil's farm. He was busy again in planting the saplings of tomatoes. Bala Patil instructed him to finish planting this evening, kicked off the bullet and went out. Yashoda went to her brother's home on the occasion before Diwali. Kalpana's elder daughter went with Yashoda for the next four days. Kalpana was busy with household chores. Her second daughter who was four years old, playing in the backyard. That was October hit & Appa continuously worked on the farm. He was fully bathed with sweat, so to take water, he came to the Bungalow & called, "Vahinisaheb please give me Tamba of water, I am thirsty now, it is too hot now, I think I have to remove my shirt", Appa mumbled.

He sat in the cowshed. Kalpana came out and handed over a Lota to him. She keenly observed Appa and said, "You must come in the room, I am giving you another shirt, this one becomes very Shaggy & clumsy".

" But it is okay! Vahinisaheb, I am working on a farm and a peasant can't work in good appearance, it is not a sahibi job" Appa smiled.

She tightly held his right hand and dragged him. "I ordered you to come and I don't want to listen to any excuses, come with me, don't say but or why".

Appa followed her, Kalpana called her daughter, "Chiu, come here", Kalpana went into the kitchen took a bowlful chane and told Appa, "You eat too and tell her to play in the backyard." Ji Vahinisaheb" Appa said with little fear.

Appa went to the backyard, and suddenly Kalpana called Appa from the bedroom, "Dattu come here fast, leave her, I need your help, come fast".

Appa shocked and ran quickly into the room, he entered into the bedroom. But Kalpana hid herself behind the door. The door was locked behind him by Kalpana. Appa moved behind & immediately closed his eyes because Kalpana was standing in front of the door without clothes, She was nude and hugged Appa tidily, Appa was shivering, he pushed Kalpana, but Kalpana's erotica did not allow her to stop. She had to climb the apex of desire, she seized back Appa again & tore his shirt. She pushed him on the bed.

After an hour, they listened to Chiu's knocking on the door. Appa woke up and dressed up. He wore the torn shirt as it was, he wanted to open the door but stopped & looked behind. Kalpana was in a sleepy mood. Appa awoke her & urged her to wear clothes because Chiu was waiting outside the door. Kalpana woke & again hugged him. "I can't leave you, "You satisfied my thirst the first time, thanks Dattu". She kissed his forehead & worn clothes and Opened the door. Chiu became bored to knock on the door, so she went to play again. Appa felt diffident. He never concentrated on his work but he had finished and without saying or looking towards Kalpana, he returned home. At the time of dinner, my mother asked him about his tattered shirt & wound mark on his ear, angrily.

Appa answered, " Shirt torn while working on a farm in the afternoon, I tried to hold a cat but she hurt me".

The first time Appa did not look into the eyes of my mother. She asked, "Has Yashoda returned to home?"

"No, she may return after a month", Appa answered.

Appa finished eating hurriedly & went out of the Juggi to sleep. She understood something because she knew Appa more than Appa knew himself. The next day Appa was working in the field & the afternoon Kalpana came into the field. "Come to home, Dattu. nobody is here, I sent Chiu to the neighbourhood. Come quickly" She held his hand & dragged him.

" But this is not fair, If Balasaheb knows he would destroy me first & then you". Appa said meticulously.

"I am already destroyed when I got married, Please give me your cherished moment", she urged in distress. Appa went with her. It had been continuously happening for up to two months. One afternoon they were in the room, and she opened the door & surprisingly, Yashoda was there. She noticed them but didn't say anything. Appa ran quickly and went home. Kalpana hastily said to her ", Dattu came to the room for cleaning".

Yashodha interrupted her, " I knew very well, this would happen one day because a kind-hearted lady cannot stay longer with her drunkard and bastard husband, She would search corner to express her, and don't worry I wouldn't say to anybody but stop it now, drunken person's brain is not in control, be careful & give a cup of tea". Kalpana shamefully touched her feet.

Yashoda changed into a benevolent person. Appa reached home in the evening in a drunkard mood, that time we were in school again. The next day, Appa did not wake up early, he felt guilty as he killed somebody, and he wanted to repent. But he heart , "Dattu, where are you?", Yashoda came to the home with Bala Patil. Appa heard & stunned. She didn't enter the Juggi, but my mother came out of the Juggi.

"Tell, Dattu to go to the farm as soon as possible because we all are going to Taluka to check Kalpana's health, She has been vomiting since midnight, & tell Dattu to clean Bangalore today as he cleaned yesterday",Yashoda ironically said.

Appa pretended to sleep but listened to everything. He woke up quickly & came out of the house, he saw Yashoda going off with Bala Patil on his bike. Appa got ready. Mother asked, "I didn't see you in a panic mood, before, I observed you in the last two months. You couldn't speak freely, you couldn't sing, and even if you didn't look into my eyes, you seemed guilty. Whatever mistake you make, forget but remember our all lives depend upon you, You are everything to me, and without you, we can't imagine our lives, whatever you are our souls, Think about us before taking any wrong step".

Appa almost in cry but he said," I promise, I won't take any wrong step, thanks to you & please forgive me",

"It's okay because sometimes life slaps us", Bear it, don't react", Mother patted him.

Yashoda took Kalpana to the taluka Hospital, The Doctor diagnosed that Kalpana was pregnant". Yashodha came to Kalpana, to congrats her. But Kalpana was in dismood and started crying, "I don't want this baby". Yashodha Patted her & took her in her lap and cajoled, "We have been blessed that we can't get our heir from Patil's blood. I assure you and behind you, You are giving us our heir, This time you will bless with a son. Forget what had happened and start your life to become a PatlianBai". They returned to home. In the afternoon, Appa fed grass to cattle and Kalpana peeped out from the window, she wanted to call him but stopped & looked at him without flickering her eyelids for a long time. Yashoda noticed her from the kitchen. The next day Yashoda called her father and sent Kalpana with her.

CHAPTER SIX

Destruction of Pink Petals

We were deeply interested in school. Our school became a real home. I enjoyed my study but Narayan was not in that mood, he was continuously talking about birds, honey, and many more Natural things. Soon a year passed I gave the class third's annual exam and in the summer our teachers dropped us at our homes. My elder sister was fourteen years old & my middle sister had taken the class six exam and was directly promoted in the next class because of her age.

When we entered the school, Soni was more attentive than me. But unfortunately, my elder sister Chanda passed only third grade in Sakhar Shala (school) a movable school which was arranged for sugar factory majdoors. That day became very hot, and that summer was troublesome. Bala Patil told Appa to find more majdoors to pluck tomatoes, the prices of tomatoes were stacked and Bala wanted to take advantage. For selling tomatoes to Surat vegetable market. He needed more majdoors & he was ready to pay seventy rupees per day. He urged Appa to take family members to pluck tomatoes.

Appa was ready & in the evening Appa told us to go to the farm. My grandmother denied it, she didn't want to send us to his farm. My grandmother hated him, but to earn money. We were ready to go with Appa, but Grandmother did not come and she told Appa not to take Chanda Di with them. Appa was ready, Mother told Chanda Di to make bhakri and green grass curry and carried food for lunch. We went in the afternoon to work even though we were twelve children to work on that farm. We wanted to earn money to buy new clothes, books, shoes & groceries and jilebi. Some of us wanted to go to watch a movie in the video parlour of Taluka.

Chanda Di came in the hot summer. She fed all of us, She was Jadugaar. There was an amazing taste in her cooking. She satisfied our hunger & returned home immediately as our grandma instructed Appa. She was merely away from the farm. Soon, Bala Patil interrupted her walk. The sun relieved its hotness every minute. The hot vapours came out from the Earth. He asked her, "Are you daughter of the Dattu?" You looked So young, but why are you going in the hot afternoon",

"Yes, Appa sent me to our home, I can't bear hard work", she answered while looking down towards Earth.

"Dattu is a rustic person, Why he called you? You are a pink Petal & you are right. A person like you was born to give orders only and not work on the farm", Bala smiled & squeezed his moustache. "Anyway I am dropping you, come and sit on my bullet", he insisted.

" No, I will go, Nobody is at home", so I will go lonely ", She shivered.

"You will become ill soon", He seized her hand & dragged her on the bike.

She didn't say something, her heart was throbbing. He started his bike and moved towards Dattu's home with her. He parked his bike in front of our Juggi. Due to summer vacation & season of cutting sugarcane, nobody was in our shoal except old Akki, because she could not move from her place, her both legs were fractured and she slept under a neem tree. She heard the throbbing voice of a bullet in front of our Juggi. Bala Patil dropped Chanda Di there & he wanted to restart his bullet soon, he called her and demanded a glass of water. She went into the Juggi as she went, Bala Patil entered the Juggi & locked the door. He Crushed the blooming pink Petal.

Before evening my grandmother returned home before us. As she returned, she noticed the condition of Chanda & suddenly came out of the home. She looked here and there & went near Akki. "Who came here? what happened ?, she asked in a trembling voice.

" I don't know but Bala Patil dropped your granddaughter and went in. I listened to her yelling loudly". Akki answered.

"Madarchoot, son of swine, I will smash that son of bitch", she muttered & moved to home. She told Chanda Tai not to open her mouth in front of anybody. She bathed her and gave her a cup of neem kadha.

We all returned home in the evening, we found Chanda was sleeping, my mother observed her keenly &

tried to wake her and also warned her not to sleep in the evening. But she didn't wake up. Grandmother told Mother, "She was shocked due to the hot summer, don't give her trouble".

Mother checked her forehead, "I am applying juice of onion on your body".

She rubbed onion & made juice, She woke up her & told her to remove her frock. As soon as she removed her frock, she was afraid & shocked to see wound marks on her body.

She hugged tightly & called grandmother, "Aatyabai look, where were you? What happened to her? Who did this? I left her in your lap", Mother cried.

As we both siblings looked at her. But that time we didn't understand what had happened to Chanda Tai, but we guessed she was suffering. Grandma consoled her & said, "Bala Patil dropped her off in the afternoon & he did the wrong thing with her, unfortunately, I was out of the home & just came before you all returned ", she sobbed. But please don't reveal anybody because she is a girl & you must know rumours of bachelor girls are spreading rapidly", and if you tell Duttu," he will kill him, so please keep mum".

Suddenly we heard the sound from the backyard, & Soni came out of the home, and Appa took out the rusty hatchet from the heap of dried Wood. He listened to the murmuring between my mother and Grandma. Soni cried but Appa moved swiftly. Suddenly both women came out of the home. They yelled to move back but Appa disappeared quickly within a moment. Grandmother called our neighbours to stop Appa. Others did not understand what had happened. One of our distant relatives enquired Akki about what had happened. because only a few families returned from daily wages. But Akki kept mum, she said nothing.

CHAPTER SEVEN

The Revenge

Appa reached Bala's Bungalow. He cried, "Where is Bala Madarchod,haramkhor ? A son of swine. I want to cut his body into pieces".

Kalpana & Yashoda came out and only looked towards him. Bala's elder daughter was afraid & hid herself in the kitchen. All the ladies looked towards him unceasingly.

Yashoda came forward & asked, "What happened Dattu? Please cool down." She was sympathetically asked.

Because both ladies understood something wrong happened. As soon as Appa opened his mouth, the roaring sound of a bullet came. Appa moved towards the bike, Hardly had the bike come near the front yard in the night, Appa forcefully hit the hatchet to Bullet, Bala fell crying under the bike, Appa lifted the bike & threw it away. He lifted Bala with full force & threw him on the floor. Appa seized the hatchet in his right hand. Here, Bala was yelling & crying. Yashoda called other people to gather. Kalpana ran towards Appa. Within a moment Appa attacked him, Bala moved but his right hand fingers cut out. Bala whined very loudly. Appa was ready to attack again on him. He lifted the hatchet in the air.

Bala saw Yamdev in Appa. Kalpana urged, "Please for the sake of my son, leave him, I am ready to do anything that you want".

Yashoda held Appa's leg, "Leave him, I promise you, you are free from all our bondages. Even I am ready to give you four acres of land, please forgive him".

Appa held that lifted hatchet in the air, he roared like a wounded tiger, "Bala don't come in front of me again, If you come that day will be the last day of your life."

"But why are you getting angry, Dattu?", Kalpana crying.

Yashoda dragged her, "Will you please shut up ?"

Yashoda saw Bala in the afternoon when he gave Chanda a lift. Now she understood everything Yashoda folded her hands & touched Appa's feet, "Please, leave him, Dattu".

Kalpana held Appa's hands in her hands, "Leave him for my son only". Appa turned back & held that hatchet & disappeared in the night.

Bala blubbered and became unconscious. Later they took him to the hospital. But never complain to the Police. Kalpana knew the next day what had happened when Yashoda scolded Bala in the hospital. Kalpana was so ashamed that she was being played the role of Bala's wife.

CHAPTER EIGHT

The Sudden Change

Appa returned home at midnight in a drunken mood. Nobody would dare to say or ask Appa what had happened. But we observed blood on the hatchet answered something dangerous. We all didn't sleep that night except Appa. The whole night we looked at each other, that hottest Summer Day burned my family. Our elder sister Chanda went through a trauma. She didn't say something, she didn't look at us, only tears came out of her eyes. We were waiting for the dawn. My grandmother took Chanda in her lap the whole night. The next morning Appa woke up & came near to Chanda. He patted her head, and a flow of tears came out of his eyes, he stood and got out of the judge.

Ramila Kaki who lived two juggis away from us came to our home. The whole community knew what had happened. But Ramila Kaki was a typical talkative lady who could not control her belly to hide secrets. She started talking with, "I think, Chanda is sick, why don't you take her to hospital?" she asked Mother in a low voice. Mother didn't pay any attention to her.

Then she turned to Grandma, "I heard Bala Patil was in the hospital, somebody cut his right-hand fingers and he was badly injured, I just told you for your information because you all were going to his farm yesterday".

My Grandmother yelled," Get out & don't come here again, you Witch, out ".

" I came here to warn all of you only, beware of that family", she ran out.

We didn't go outside the juggi that day. I didn't understand what had happened but I understood that something bad happened with my Chanda didi. I was the only person who did not know about the incident. At night, Appa returned with Mama, and both declared that Chanda's marriage would held in the next week.

" But, she is not ready yet, for marriage," Grandma said in a low voice.

"She is quite enough mature, her mother was the same age when she married me. The Groom is hamal in an onion market of taluka, he earns enough. He had a pakka house in the river area. He has one girl & a son. His wife died two years ago during pregnancy, He is the most suitable person for her. One more thing he knows everything about what had happened. And he is ready to accept her. So, this is my final decision, and I don't allow anyone to change it, I did not take any decision about you all but this is my final verdict, get ready her, tomorrow we will go to the Taluka market to purchase new clothes & marriage ceremony material, one more thing nobody will tell anyone about it. We will go to the Chanda's mama's home, where we will celebrate marriage & don't talk about around us about Chanda's marriage,"Appa threatened all of us.

The next day we all packed our luggage. We first walked towards the taluka market, Appa and Aai purchased Nauwvari & clothes & Rukhwat. In the evening, we reached Mama's village. We all were verbatim of Appa's words even Grandmother's could not dare to go beyond his words. The day before her marriage for the mandav day. Mama's front yard is decorated with the branches of mango, guava, odumber, jamun & neem trees. In the evening all women were invited to perform Chanda Didi's Pooja. Then I applied Holy turmeric powder &gulabjal on her face. She wore a yellow saree for the first time. She looked like an angel but a pale angel. She looked so beautiful but a peaceful lady. One of the ladies gave her a 10 rupee note in her hand and touched her head with folding fingers.

"I haven't seen such a beautiful Pari in my life, you look so pretty & blessed with heavenly beauty," What's your name? If you meet me earlier, I will choose you as my daughter-in-law, Do you have any sibling sisters of your age? Tell me ?", she asked curiously.

She became mousy so she was unable to speak. Chanda Di did not give any expression. Her life became tedious. Even the guests urged her to smile. She stood like a statue. One of the old women whispered in another woman's ear, "Her marriage is fixed with a widower person that's why she looks nervous, if I knew about her before, I would arrange this marriage with my nephew in a precious lounge, anyway, ApnaApnaNaseeb", Chanda Di stood dumbly.

The next day, everyone was yearnelywaired for marriage except Chanda Di, At that time I realised marriage means the death of a teenage girl & birth of a responsible woman. The ceremony was over. At the time of farewell, Chanda Di cried from her heart, even I think she did not understand about her marriage, she was a mute spectator and accepted everything like a typical Indian girl from the Aadivasi area.

We returned home after a week until then everyone knew about Didi's marriage. In the evening everyone came to home to congratulate us from the bottom of their hearts. Because such a kind of catastrophe was not new to them. In every family, having a girl faced such a trauma. But that was very shocking for us that changed our life. Appa declared that Soni would not attend school from the moment.

Grandma said, "She is safer in school than living with us, You must know living alone in our community destroys a woman's life. She is not quite mature at least she should spend the next few years in a school. I left my doll just for three hours & that hours destroyed our lives. So, Dattu for God's sake send her school".

The next morning, Appa told us to get ready for school. We prepared & Appa left us at Ashram School.

Now, he returned home and sat in front of both ladies. Grandma said, "It is very hard to live without children at home they are angels of happiness, I can't live without Chanda, she was my doll, Why did you declare her marriage? Dattu, I hate you, you are also an offender".

Appa spoke with tears in his eyes, "You know very well, how I loved all of you, first. I am a father and I love my children more than my life. How would I see my daughter's suffering? You know the news about her would spread all over and it would become very hard for a seduced girl to survive peacefully. I know that she was in a great trauma. But the best way to overcome it was marriage only. She would forgive her catastrophe in a year, the bridegroom was a vegetarian, he would look after her and the most important thing, he knew everything about her although he was happy to accept her. He is the most understanding person, he will keep our child happy there", Appa confidently said.

Now both are relieved from tension. Mother asked," But how would we survive? What would we do for our livelihood? "The day after tomorrow, you and me going to join sugarcane labourers and Aai will live here, she wouldn't sustain with us, we will send some money for her living," Appa said.

" But I will accompany all of you, I can't live without you" she declared. That day Mother made Bhakri and dal, all ate with full of stomach.

In the next morning, "Dattu, Dattu, is anyone in the home ?", Yashoda called.

"Who is there ?" mother asked,

" I am Yashoda and Kalpana is also with me", Why are you both here? first time mother yelled in an angry mood.

"We want to talk with him", Kalpana said.

Appa woke up and called both in the home."What do you want?" Appa asked rudely.

"We are here to return your land and here are the documents", Kalpana said softly and continuously steering towards him."And you are free from all bondages now, "she said and smiled.

"And for gaining this freedom I paid my daughter's flesh, am I right? I won't come to your farm because your man destroyed my Pari's life and that burned my heart. I know myself very well that I will finish him whenever I see him. Even I wouldn't like to return my land because we are heirs of Eklavya the Veer from Mahabharata. We are very stuck with our words and people will say, that Dattu broke his bondages from Patil's clutches by exchanging his daughter's flesh. Now I want your last Upkar, don't come into our life."Appa folded his hands.

"But you can improve your life by taking your land", Kalpana urged.

"You are returning me everything because you are repenting, I have a request please don't show your faces again, keep away from us", Appa said.

Yashoda stood & held Kalpana's hand, " I have already told you, Majdoor cannot change their kismat of majdoori", and they went. The next morning came with new rays of hope. Appa hired Oxen & Oxford and March towards the sugarcane factory. The season of cutting sugarcane crops started in October and ended in June. He joined the labour force in January.

CHAPTER NINE

The Catastrophe

Some years passed rapidly, I was in Eight classes. On 15th August midnight, the day we celebrated our independence. I slept but Naru woke me at midnight he said, "I feel suffocated, I think my mother is calling me, I never felt like before, Please help me to go out, I want to go home now".

"Ok, cool down, We will go in the morning with taking permission from the proctor", I patted him.

He responded, " But I didn't feel like this, I have to go, tell me, you help me or not, otherwise I am eloping".

He took his school bag & made it empty, he filled his bag with the toasts, which we received two toasts in every morning. We stored one toast every day, when we felt hungry, we ate.

"Now I am going", he came out of the room, there was a stunned silence in the building.

" Stop, I am with you, don't panic," I told him.

And I wore my uniform because we didn't have more clothes but we had two uniforms. We came backyard of the building, there was a six-foot wall compound. Suddenly, I remembered we kept a ladder near the flag post. I secretly took that ladder and we climbed on the wall & jumped outside. We started our journey towards Narayan's village at midnight but Naru's favourite friend, Nature denied us not to go to the village.

Abruptly the Storm Started, Lightning was roaring and showing anger at us but it showed the road in the night. The day was Amavasya. I feared but Naru didn't want to stop, he started running, he was not in the mood to listen, he just followed him & I didn't remember, where we were going. I didn't remember the road, direction and situation. Even Naru could not understand the way, but he was saying repeatedly, My mother is calling me, she is calling, she is in dangered, maybe she is sick, I want to meet her as soon as". He never stopped, even our legs were wounded due to thorns, broken glasses and sharpened stones. But his attention was only on his mother. Suddenly, the heavy rainfall started but his desire was stronger than any rainfall. We reached his village but his local river did not allow us to go home. The river flowed fast but Naru dived into the river he neither thought about me nor looked. I followed him & he dived, I dived behind him, within a few minutes we were on the next side.

Now, Naru started running faster than before, I never tried to stop him. We reached his home early in the morning. We crossed fifty km in just eight to nine hours.

The rain stopped now, and people gathered around his house. We saw some people were busy in making a bamboo ladder, anyone's last bed. One of them turned towards Naru, " Who told you about this ?, How you come?

Naru asked, "What happened?". People looked towards him without saying anything.

He found the way into the crowd & entered the home, he was stunned & yelled, "Aai, look at me. I am here, Wake up and make me Sheera, I am so hungry." He sat and toppled on his mother's body. Her body was covered with a white dhoti. A couple of cotton were packed in her nostrils. Naru removed cotton from her nose. Two adult men came & grabbed him. They tightly held him, he became unconscious. I was shocked. He loved his mother as much as I did.

I remember as she came to meet Naru first time, Naru introduced me to her. She hugged me affectionally as I felt she was like my mother. She gave me guavas & told me, " You must stay with him like a brother". I touched her head there was a wound mark. I tried to ask her but I stopped. In the evening I asked Naru, What happened with Mavshi?

Naru answered in distress," My father was drunk. He beat my mother every day and she bore him only because of me and my sister".

His father killed his mother in a drunken mood that night when she was busy with household chores. His father entered the house taking a sharp sickle in his hand and came near her.

He grabbed her hair and asked, "Who did you meet in the evening?" Without opening her mouth, he cut her throat with a sharp sickle and laid her in blood. The next morning, police arrested him.

Naru was uncontrolled, he cried & yelled from the bottom of his heart. Even I was so shocked to see her body in white shrewd. I was crying loudly. I realised the most heaviest burden on us is the body of our family members. His mother's body was buried in the jungle side. I grabbed his hands & took him into the house. In the evening, his all relatives went away. Nobody would be ready to stay there. Only one of his neighbours Aunty bought a Bhakari & kadhi for him. He was in trauma. I told him to eat, he didn't want to say, he steered towards that place where his mother's body was kept. He stood & again toppled on that place & crying. His throat became sore due to continuous crying and he didn't take water since we eloped. Now, he became unconscious. I was afraid & came out of the home. I saw that neighbour's aunty who gave us food. I called her. She woke him & gave him a glass full of milk.

She consoled him & told me, " His father did not allow him to anyone come here", he was a suspiciously minded person, even I was afraid of who will take care of his siblings because nobody would dare to look after them".

She went after feeding us. His mother had an empty house only a few utensils were there. I did not see clothes, groceries or necessary things. Because his father sold everything to drink Daaru. His mother was a little literate. That's why she sent her children to school & I got my brother a friend. She knew only education could save her children from labouring. Otherwise, his father opposed her decision to take education. He wanted to send his children to labour to gain money for drinking. The next day, we closed the doors of juggi. He did not lock the room.

CHAPTER TEN

New Home

Naru was hanged, I took him towards my home because Appa and others were at home in August. We started our marching towards my home. We reached at home midnight. I knocked on the door, Appa opened the door & he seized my collar and slapped me. After eloping we became truants & our teacher came to our home for enquiry.

After beating me, he stopped and said, "You are my last hope dear, Why you deceived me? "Why did you elope without informing anyone?", Give me the answer.

Naru came forward and folded his hands, “Please stop uncle, he eloped with me, I wanted to meet my mother & when we reached, she died, my father killed her. Please don’t beat my brother, he did it for my sake".

Appa was stunned and ashamed of his behaviour, "I am so sorry dear, I did not know reality".

Meanwhile, my Grandma and mother came due to clamorous. Appa told everything to Aai. My mother embraced him. Naru felt his mother appeared before him. He was smiling & delighted. He asked, "May I call you Mai? I feel & see my mother within you”.

“Oh! Sure, you are my son, Now," Mother replied affectionally, “You both look hungry, I am making Shira for both of you". That day Naru satisfied his hunger in his new home.

CHAPTER ELEVEN

Fight with Draught

After two days Appa left us at school. Time ran fast, Naru and his sister because part & parcel of our family. Naru and my sister Soni passed matriculation with first class. That was a sign of their career ending in an education field. We moved to the next class, One day an officer from the social welfare department came to our school for career guidance. He wanted to guide the scheduled Tribe candidate in the Armed Forces. Students must move towards Armed forces & State Police forces because the ratio of this community is very low in Armed forces. According to his survey, Adivasis were a monolithic homogeneous community & that's why they were not sustained in the Armed forces. Mostly they eloped from the forces. He pursued us towards Defence.

He carried a film projector with him & showed us the film "Prahar". I was highly inspired by Nana Patekar as a soldier & I decided to become a soldier. I revealed my dream to Naru but Naru was not interested in it. He said "I am afraid of bullets & guns, If you go in defence, anyone can shoot you, my neighbour's uncle said, " Soldier is a very dangerous person, to become a soldier you have to cut your fingers and eat swine every day with cooking their meat. Sometimes you must eat dogs & bitches".

I laughed at his innocence sense. He said, " We will become police, a Dada Manus ."

I nodded & firmly told him, "I will go in the Indian army".

He argued with me & finally said, "Ok, wherever & whenever you go, I will follow you but Only for yourself."

The officer from social welfare also explained the entries of ladies in Police forces & their reservations. I wanted to tell my sister Soni about the police force. During Diwali vacation, we wanted to go home but Appa and all our family members already moved towards sugar factories at Gujrat. He sent us a message that we must stay in school during the Diwali vacation. I was very curious about Diwali vacation because Diwali came with new clothes & my favourite firecracker. This time, I would not get that. Because Appa knew his responsibility, our family became a large family for feeding and livelihood. Appa had to work hard. The factories of sugarcanes from Gujrat were giving higher wages than Maharashtra. We stayed at school, there was only a couple of cook, They fed us and we kept neat and clean the premises and classroom. To keep clear the surroundings became part of my daily routine. Diwali Vacations finished & summer vacations came. This time we were fortunate to live with family members. I told Soni &Manisha Tai about women recruitment in the police forces. Both girls were ready to join but my Grandmother Stopped them, She advised Appa to tie their knots soon. But Soni Tai argued that she had to look recruitment process. Appa gave her a positive response. I had already taken the postal address of the social welfare officer. I wrote to the officer to inform us about the recruitment Rally of police forces especially for ladies. In the second month of May, We received a letter from that officer. That was the first letter which I received first time in my life. He informed us about the recruitment rally to be held on the last Sunday of May at Nashik police ground. We must keep ready with documents. Soon, Appa steered to collect the necessary documents of school L.C, Caste Certificate & domicile certificate also Dongari certificate.

Manisha Tai also wanted to join but Appa failed to gain her caste certificate and domicile certificate. She became so nervous and on the other side was very much curious about Soni Tai. On that particular day, Soni Tai & Appa went to Nashik police ground. A mass crowd was there. There were separate lines of girls. The lines were divided according to caste and religion. Soni Tai's documents were verified. The security persons did not allow Appa to enter the ground. The lady police guard measured Soni Tai's chest & height. She was physically fit & moved towards running. Around two hundred girls were selected for running. The group of girls was ready to run. Some girls pushed Soni Tai back, and soon one of the lady constables observed she did not wear running shoes. She stopped Soni Tai and enquired. Tai answered, "It is not affordable for us to purchase shoes".

"But you may get injured, because the whole ground becomes a hot pan", she said.

"Whatever will happen, but I have to run." Soni Tai confidently responded.

"Best luck dear, I wanted to check your desire, "See you soon in the ward", the lady constable told her.

On a very hot summer afternoon, the race started. Soni Tai was charged with power and trying to lead the group. But the first three girls did not give her space to overtake. But before the finishing line, she crossed all the girls & grabbed first position. She achieved first position in every task even in the written examination & appeared for a medical test on the next day. That day, both Appa & Soni Tai lived beside the ground. Soni Tai cleared her medical test on the next day & selected as a police constable. The Supretended Of Police addressed all the selected candidates & congratulated them.

He instructed selected cadets," Your training will start in the next month, until then you can go home, rest & enjoy because you won't get too much time to spend with your family. You have to do your duty 24 hours. This is our devotion towards our country. You are very much fortunate that you become part of the best police force in India."

He examined the selected candidates's list & called Soni Tai. He was highly appreciated by Soni Tai's efforts & gave her a bouquet. Appa observed that moment from the gate of the police ground. Soni Tai hugged Appa and touched his feet. Soon they reached our home after three days. The news got viral in the village and the whole community came to congratulate us. But sometimes, Nature does not take favour of workable people.

The month of June passed. There was not a single sign of rain. We already suffered due to drought. The whole area of farming became drastic, the birds left, and trees became dried. No one could see a greeny and shady tree. Farmers sold their cattle at a very cheap rate. Appa did not want to sell the oxen, because the oxen were used to carry sugarcane. They were the source of our bread & butter. That night Appa did not sleep & went to the backyard to talk with his oxen. I and Naru observed Appa. Even the school started on 14 June but due to drought school principal refused to take us.

Appa muttered to himself, "I won't let you go or die, don't worry my friends." The oxen shook their heads and tails.

Appa disappeared that night. We moved into our home. Mother told me to call Appa. I answered her that he had gone somewhere. We went to bed in the night. But my mother did not sleep. Appa entered the home in the dawn.

"Where were you roaming in the whole night?", Mother asked.

"I never roamed somewhere, I took a walk, a night walk", He answered.

"I think, it was a huge night walk, which took several hours of night."Mother cleverly said.

"Oh! don't ask me", He interrupted.

She stood & went backyard, The oxen were enjoying the green grass while raising their tails in the air. My mother understood & returned to him, "I knew, you would do something for our members, but what about tomorrow, "You can't feed them every day, because here we can't sustain ourselves for more than two days," she said in distressed.

"Don't worry God is kind, he will show us the way. Please make me something to eat," Appa said.

"There is nothing to eat, edible oil has finished and we can't purchase."Mother muttered.

Naru was keenly listening. He came near Aai & said, "Don't worry Mai, God is great, Lord Hanuman will give a way, I am going to his temple and today is Saturday".He escaped rapidly and returned in the afternoon.

He handed over a plastic bag full of edible oil to Mai, "Mai here take this oil, use it up to a whole week, I will give you another pouch in the next week", Naru told his mother touching his right hand to his shirt collar.

“Did you steal?” Mother inquired.

He added, "Please Mai don't ask me from where I bought it, I just say, this is given by God Hanuman to me, believe me."

Mother accepted without grumbling. We struggled the gain food, grass & water. We didn't have money & work, it was a time to survive on tree leaves or roots. The farmers and peasants relieved their cattle. That night our people came together, and one of the older people Bhalu called all of us, he said," Soon, we are facing problems of food & water, we have to survive. For it, we will leave this area within the next few days, I am requesting all of you to search for a better place for habitation. We will move there as soon as possible as I heard the southern area has greenery and enough water bodies. But nobody from that area is ready to give a place in the region. If we get at least an acre of land to live we would survive up to rain coming, Now we found two dead sheep we are making pieces for all of us. But don't waste water for washing hands, toilet or anywhere except drinking. We will carry out this until we get new accommodation."

We all ate together that night except my family because my grandma had already arranged pulses, jaggery, and flour for us. And She told my mother to keep it secret.

In the early morning of Saturday Naru woke up before us. He applied ash on his forehead and wore Saffron cloth as a turban on his head. He made that Saffron cloth from a tearning old tattered shirt. He marched, I was observing him and followed him secretly. He reached the Maruti Temple after walking five miles. That was a holy place where people visited to fulfil their wishes. People performed Pooja and conferred coconut and a small pouch of oil with salt, chilly. Some people offered direct oil into the large stone lamp, some gave jaggery and bhakari even some of them threw coins there. The architecture of the ancient temple was built in the HemadPanthi style. People believed that Lord Hanuman stayed there for some days to do Tapa.

Naru entered the temple. He swiped the temple and premises with the branches of the Banyan Tree. The sacred tree stood behind the temple. He sat near the statue of Lord Hanuman and went into Samadhi. I came near the gate of the temple but did not dare to disturb him. I moved towards home to inform them that Naru was engaged in working somewhere. In the late night, Naru returned with a load of sack on his head. He called to help Appa and Appa lifted the sack from his head. It was full of cracked coconuts, jaggery, bhakri, chana and small pouches of oil. He took out chillers from his pocket and handed them over to mother and said, "We can survive at least a week on it."

Appa got angry and wanted to slap him but he controlled himself because he thought, he did not have the right to do it. He moved out of the home immediately.

Mother summoned Naru, "It is not good to steal things from God, God will curse us, you must return it dearly, we are not beggars."

"But these things would be wasted even if dogs entered the temple and spoiled these things. We are human, we need it for survival and God is kind, if Lord Hanuman did not want to give me, he could have stopped me but he did not do that and he allowed me to carry the things please, accept it. If my mother lived on time, she would accept it. And I can't force you all because you fed us, siblings," Naru cleverly answered.

Mother failed to argue with him. She convinced Appa later about Naru's deed.

CHAPTER TWELVE

The Shabari Dham

The next morning one rowdy person enquired about Naru. He came over home. We all sat in the front yard of the home. It was nearly 8 o'clock but the sun from the East side was showering fire on everyone. The person came near us and inquired to Appa about Naru. Naru slept at home. Mother thought the person belonged to the Maruti temple & he was looking for Naru to punish him for his deed. The person was a stranger & asked about Naru. My neighbours came to near him. One of our neighbours told him. He may sleep at home. Without taking permission. The Stranger entered my home. He woke Naru. We followed him.

Naru awoke with rubbing his eyes, "Kaka, Are you here? What happened ?"

"Thank God, you recognise me, I have been searching for you since last week, I went to your school and I got the address. I am sorry for whatever happened. I am sorry that you are living with the strangers but I have to repent, Your mother fed & grew me when I was a child. She was more than vahini to me. She was my mother. Now I come to take you both." He explained in fervency

"But this is my family now uncle, I can't leave them, they all supported me in my bad days. How can I leave them on dangerous days?", Naru replied.

"Whatever but Naru, I am ready to give the money and food to them but you must live with us?" " Uncle urged.

"Sorry dear uncle, There is no way, we must stay with them until their last days. Now, they are my parents," Naru responded.

"Ok ! Then I am giving you a five-acre land of our forefathers. I didn't hand it over to your father because he would sell that land one day at a cheap rate for Daru. But it is a time to take your land. It is near ShabriDham in Saputara range. It is 70 km away from it. The land is holy and blessed by Lord Shri Ram, Lakshman, Hanuman & Devi Shabri. It is rich with plenty of water, Jungle and fertile soil. You can go and stay there. I am giving the documents to you. You should move from here as early as possible. I am waiting for you and the family", Uncle said.

Appa interrupted their communication and said, "You can take Naru and Mangal with you, we are not ready to leave this place because, we are not selfish, if we leave our people in danger, God won't forgive us".

"So, Why don't you all move to the Shabari Dham jungle area? There is a pond of crystal water. The jungle is fully reached with various fruit trees, birds & hares. I am the Sarpanch of that area, I will give you all entry into my region and for your livelihood. I will provide you with the opportunities from Rojgar Hami Yojana", he insisted.

Appa was ready & moved to the next lane to summon people around us. Within a few minutes, people gathered around Appa. Appa told them about the place, and journey and ordered all to pack everything to move. Around 200 members agreed with him & started packaging. In the afternoon we all were ready to walk seventy k.m. We all kept only necessary things in our Gathode. But Sony Tai refused to come with us. When Appa asked her, She said, "I will receive my Police Bharti appointment this month. How can I leave? the postman will carry the letter and if I won't to join the force on time with a letter. I will disqualify."

Appa persuades her, "Don't worry, dear... The Postman is my friend, he will inform us there. I am giving him our new destination".

Soni Tai Smiled. Our hode arranged ten oxfords for carrying loads and belongings. All elders were instructed to use fords and wagons for carrying children & pregnant women. We started our marching in the late afternoon & walked up to 20 k.m. The next day, up to the late night we reached the destination. Naru's uncle warmly welcomed us and showed us the habitat for living. Our people raised the trampoline tents there. We were starting our lives like refugees.

The next morning, we were impressed by the surrounding Nature. Nature enticed us & induced us to live. There was clamorous in the morning. We found a pond very near to our habitat. First time in a month our men & women were running to bathe, and children sat around the pond for scatting. There was hovering to fetch water. Appa and Bhalu Kaka had instinctively come forward to the crowd & appealed to all.

Appa roared, "Remember & come forward here, this is our asylum, we must control our behaviour, this is a holy place & we are guests here. No one should throw garbage, or bags here & there. No one goes to directly bating in the pond. Even women must not wash clothes and utensils near it. We have to use crystal water for drinking purposes. The sarpanch was allowed to live here for some days. He will not acclaim us, If our conduct is abnormal. The locals abused us. The locals & Sarpanch advocated for us means not, we are taking benefits according to our ways. We are straightforward persons & would not want to become a part of a boycott. We have been facing calamity for the last two months & do not have a desire to go into exile again without water. The environment is an endowment for us. We must give respect to this hallowed place".

All moved silently into the tents. That day, the sarpanch gave us the feast of Khichdi and continue it for the next two days. Meanwhile, he offered males & females the work from Rojgar Hami Yojna. Men and women went to construct dams near the Jungle. We past seven days. Naru's uncle showed us the piece of land, that belonged to Naru. It was very much near to our habitat. There was a well on the farm. Appa decided to stay there. On the Eighth day, the Postman came & called Soni Tai. Soni Tai was busy with Mangal in reading books. She heard the sound of the Postman & ran towards Dackman. He handed over a letter of training and she had to report after the next 10 days. She was delighted after all she was the first person from my family to join a government job. The news rapidly spread in our confraternity. Everyone congratulated Soni Tai & Appa.

Appa was so happy & told Soni Tai, " I badly treated Chanda, I dreamed that Chanda would get a government officer, but it was ok, Sometimes things do not change according to our desire, we must have changed ourselves," I feel guilty for her".

"But Appa she is happy with her family and I will fulfil your desire, I will help my youngers to get government jobs. I will help them financially", Soni Tai opened her mind.

Appa had decided to give all the grand feast of masala rice to everyone. To make a feast, he ordered all of us to collect dried wood for chula. We all siblings were busy collecting dried Wood. Appa warned us not to go deep into the Jungle.

Soni Tai & Mangal Tai went to collect wood from the Jungle. Mangala Tai climbed on a Pimpal tree & cut the dried branches with a sharp sickle. Soni Tai was busy collecting dried branches under the tree. Suddenly, Mangala Tai cried from the tree, "Soni run, run fast!... Here is a tiger," Soni was buffled & turned around, soon within a second tiger jumped on her and severed her head & ran towards Jungle.

Soni Tai didn't get time to move somewhere nor Mangal Tai succeeded in saving her. Mangal Tai became unconscious to see the blood & shivering bloody body without a head. She collapsed on a tree on the floor.

We heard the clamorous & thought that Mangala might fall on the tree. I ran to call Appa & Naru towards the direction. Naru reached there, he was horrified to see the body of Soni Tai. The legs and hands of the body were fluttering fast & a splash of blood was scattering. He moved towards our tents and dragged a saree of Mother, which was hanged for drying. He took it & came, he overspreaded that saree on the body. We all reached the spot.

Appa yelled at Naru, ..." Who is lying under the saree? somebody, remove the cloth,...... who is behind it..... ?"

Mangal Tai was roaring from another side, ...'Tiger, Tiger!, tiger severed her head, somebody saves her", she became unconscious again.

Appa looked and courageously removed the clothes, Naru cuddled him & tried to stop him but Appa pushed him away. He removed the saree, everyone was shocked to see the Splash of blood & body without a head. Some of us Shivered, I yelled loudly & put my head on the near tree. Appa sat down & lifted body mutely & moved.

He muttered, "Today I am giving a feast for my dear, on behalf of your selection in the police force. You are the first girl from our community to enter in police. I will stitch you new Khaki, black leather shoes and salute. I will arrange your marriage with the government officer".

Appa lifted her body in his arms and moved towards our tents. The whole gathering followed him with mourning. He came centre of a tent. My mother fainted to see the heartbreaking view. The dark cloud gathered and light thrashed and the cloud started raining. The rain wiped out the splash of blood. The clouds burst water heavily as they were mourning. That day rain poured water up to the next morning. We were mourning in our tent. The rain stopped in the next morning. Sarpanch came and alerted us not to stay there because the pond nearby us was already overloaded and flood could enter at any moment. Some of the four people dug a graveyard on Naru's farm. We buried Soni Tai there because we failed to burn her body. Bhalu Kaka instructed all to wrap our belongings. They all kept belongings in the oxfords. Even Bhalu Kaka grabbed the hand of Appa & settled him in an Oxford. Appa became motionless. Our whole family sat in the Oxford. Appa muttered,...... "I have lost my both daughters, one was mentally dead & another physically. What a punishment I have received!"

CHAPTER THIRTEEN

Lost of Hope

We didn't remember how we all reached our own homes. How was Mangla Tai with us? How did the week pass? But the rain had already occupied our region. We became a part of everyone's compassion. Nature brutally suppressed us. After a few days, our school teachers came to pick up us. Appa sent me & Naru to school that was my last year in the school. We were in matriculation. The year was very crucial to me. I didn't concentrate on my study. As I thought, I had spent many years searching for myself and I had forgotten about school & education. That year, a social welfare officer came to counsel us for a guiding career. They showed us a PPT presentation about the streams after SSC. They introduced us Arts, Commerce & Science streams. They explained the ways of entering Engineering, Medical, government services, cooperative services etc. Even they calculated the years. But I remember how last year an officer guided us about the Armed Forces, the shortest way to enter government bureaucracy.

I told myself, I would like to see myself in Army uniform as a soldier. On the day of Dussehra Appa and other members moved to the sugarcane factory. I felt Naru was quite more mature than me. He encouraged me to study. He didn't allow me to swipe our room. He fetched water for me, he washed my clothes. He became an essential part of my life. I took the first position and gained 90% in the first-semester examination. Our final examination was started on the third of March. In the evening of our first paper, one of the boys knocked on the door, I was busy taking notes, so I left my place but Naru stopped me and opened the door, that boy whispered in his ears.

"Janya ! I think my uncle has come to meet me, I am going outside to meet him, you should continue your studies, "Naru advised me.

" I want to meet your uncle, I am coming with you, " please!, I interrupted.

He refused & said, "Sorry he called me to share some secrets, and please don't follow me". He went.

I Peeped out the door and from a distance. I observed him he hugged a stranger person in the darkness. I didn't see clearly but I was sure that the person was not his uncle. I turned back and dived into books, I studied up to 2 o'clock in the night, but I didn't concentrate on my studies. Now, this time. I felt suffocated & my mind was continuously thinking about Appa. I was very much curious about to meet him. Even I sensed that Appa came to meet me.

He sat near me and patted my head. "Jana, you are my only hope dear, you can break the bondage. I must see you to join government Services. You become an idol in front of our shoal. You must guide them to overcome poverty. You know the calculation of poverty starts from our birth and it adheres to us up to our death. Nobody from us would dare to break the chain of poverty except your Soni Tai. She was brave but destiny never allowed her to cross the line, I was very much afraid of you, but I have confidence that you will wipe the line of poverty. I am always with you, you must remember that whenever you feel, you can't win the situation just close your eyes, and think about all of us and what happened in our past. You will get the ways." Appa disappeared after convincing me.

But I felt like Naru when he felt about her mother on that certain day. I closed my eyes and saw my family, I was with Soni Tai, Appa and Chanda Didi. We were laughing and playing Vitti Dandu together. Appa heated the Vitti far away and we siblings yelled loudly.

Soon, Naru woke up me, " Get up Jana ! Within an hour the exam starts, get ready for the exam."

I distressedly said, "Naru, I have to go to meet Appa, I don't want to give an exam".

"It's okay we will go to meet him, but remember, what is Appa's dream? Have you forgotten? His only hope is you dear. Keep concentrating on studyin,." Naru told me as I thought my Appa convinced me.

I solved my paper on time. The exam was tough but I faced it smartly. Before my last paper in the evening, I packed my & Naru's belongings & luggage. As soon as the paper finish, we had to move towards the sugarcane factory to meet all. The paper was over, I was ready to start my journey towards the factory with Naru. But Naru insisted that we had to move our home because the whole family returned home.

I asked, "How should you know about it? Are you sure our family returned home".

Naru answered in a low voice, " Yes and we should directly go home."

The school arranged a truck for all of us to leave at our homes. During the journey I conversed with Naru, " Appa missed Soni Tai very much, Naru. Before the first paper, Appa came to meet me, Now I am going towards Appa, like you were thinking continuously for your mother".

Naru retorted, "Sometimes we must be ready for unwanted calamity, sometimes we didn't expect the unwanted eruption would bandish us, sometimes we can't be ready to accept destiny's decision and sometimes we can't accept how life turns fast on another way".

" Why you are explaining me like a philosopher? I think you hid some clandestine things & since the first paper evening, I have observed you & realised you are very talkative but you didn't speak more than four words from that day. What happened?, Please, why I didn't feel pleasurable after covering the examination", I said unpleasantly.

Naru responded, "You can't bear dear".

" But what? Which catastrophe came, I think it would not more than the loss of Soni Tai, "I told him.

Naru said, " Yes it is more than that we have lost Appa before our paper, your guess was right, The person came with that news.... that night".

The person said, "Dattu loaded a truck of sugarcane before evening, he got extra money from Mukadam. He returned to his tent every evening early. But people from his confraternity took illicit power supply from the nearest electric poles, every evening they hung a wire with dried bamboo on the electric pole. They circulated their turns. That day rain dropped and the bamboo they used to tangle the power supply wire moistened. That was Bhalu Kaka's turn, but he went to hospital for her wife's stomachache. And so Dattu tried to do his work. Dattu was against it but he went to carry Bhalu Kaka's duty. He was to be absorbed in thoughts of Soni Tai. He took bamboo without applied dried clothes around it, that was Amavasya and others could not see clearly in the evening. As soon as he touched the bamboo to the main supply wire, the wire sparked with lightning and it banged Appa mercilessly & he hurled up to twelve feet away. His back head collided with the stone. He took his last breath there. The heavy rainfall came down the whole night in the region that was unwanted rain. There were neither dark clouds nor a sign of rain".

Naru continued, "Bhalu Kaka and others carried his body to our home. They burned Appa, there Mangla Tai performed the last rites. Since then our whole family lived there. I know you can't forgive me but I was following only the last wish of our Appa. He was also my father even more than a father. I didn't receive love from my father, I think I am a bad patch for your family. Appa lost his wife while carrying family burden and I was in a dilemma for not to reveal the truth..."

I grabbed his collar and slapped him continuously for not telling the truth. He was responsible for not allowing me to do the last rites of Appa. The other students and my Maths teachers in the truck had been listening without interrupting.

My teacher seized me, "Control yourself, dear, he was not peccant, he is merely a puppet in the hands of Destiny. Don't blame him, he is your real friend, You have already lost your father but don't lose your friend now".

Naru sat silently holding his head between folded legs. The truck dropped us to our home. Without waiting to take my luggage, I ran towards my home. It was already a month passed. I entered the home, mother sat quietly in a corner. She was continuously looking towards Appa's hippy cut photos. I spotted her forehead and could not bear her forehead without Bindiya and Kumkum. I knew that I had lost the most precious person of my life my Appa, my shadow of God. But I didn't have time to sink in mourning. The burden of responsibility came on my shoulders. I turned back and enquired Mangala Tai about Grandmother. She informed me that she went to get help from her friends. Grandmother returned in the evening with empty hands.

She talked with her mother, "I don't realise that I am an old lady now, I can't gain money and work but can gain sympathy only, my well-wisher left the world! and I am that lady who didn't engage in hard work and I can't beg, I will prefer death than begging."

Naru and I listened to the emotional expressions of my ladies. I told Naru, "From tomorrow I will go to Taluka market with Bhalu Kaka for Hamali on daily wages, you must stay at home with them."

Naru responded, "There is no need to go outside the home, my uncle is coming tomorrow, I am signing the deal with him, he needs my land for the next five years, for poultry farming and milk production and in reverse he is ready to give me five thousand for a year. I think this is enough for our survival ".

"But Naru, that amount is yours, we are not your shareholders," I told him.

He sarcastically laughed at me, "You tell me, what is yours and what is mine? I called all our family and you are separating us, We are siblings. If Appa was alive, he wouldn't push me out of family and if you think we are not part of the family, we both leave home tomorrow forever",Naru retorted.

I didn't have words to argue with my brother. The next day Naru took five thousand from his uncle and handed it over to Mai.

Soon, after the matriculation result was declared, my principal Shinde sir and Marathi teacher Gaikwad sir came home with a kilo Pedha. I gained ninety-three per cent and secured first rank in a district. While Naru gained sixty-two per cent. The principal congratulated me and others. I offered a Pedha in front of Appa and tears flowed out from my eyes. I thought every time Nature or destiny, whatever can't bear our happiness. They are searching the ways to break our chain of happiness. Gaikwad sir captured my image in his Kodak camera for record and giving news in the newspaper. They promised me to guide for college education. My principal sir told me to go to Taluka College to be admitted to the 11th class. He gave me a bona fide certificate, L.C and a special recommendation letter for admission. Naru's name was also mentioned there. They left and disappeared. I realised the role of teachers in our lives. That was praiseworthy.

CHAPTER FOURTEEN

College Life

We two went to take admission to Taluka College and fixed it. We took admission in 11th Arts. The college was twelve k.m. away from our destination. It was on our way to Taluka. On the very first day, we walked barefoot to college. Our hearts were running speedily while entering the class. We sat on the last benches. The class was full of hundred and fifteen boys & only five girls with various fashions. The sons of Marwadis, traders, police officers, and landlords occupied the first lines. The first lecture was in English. The English Teacher entered the classroom with Hollywood attire. He impressed all of us but in the first side. He was not only good-looking but a knowledgeable person. Very soon, our class introduction started, and everyone introduced themselves in their mother tongue. When my turn came I introduced myself with Naru in English. The whole class dragged attention towards me.

The teacher said, " I read your news in the newspaper, if I am not wrong, you gained the first position in our district, right".

"Yes sir, I answered".

"Why did you seek admission in the Arts stream instead of science?", He questioned.

Sir, my dream is to join the government sector as soon as and for it I will enter in Armed forces as a soldier",I smartly answered.

The sound of claps dumbed my ears. Aher sir our English teacher, my idol in the next life suggested to me," If you have the ability & ready to hard work, why do you think to enter as a Soldier, pull a big target dear, try for NDA, as brighter students think brighter, you must concentrate on becoming an officer, I will direct you, I am an NCC officer and I am in search of a student like you. Who are deeply haunted to serve in the Armed forces, from today you must communicate with me in English, and I will give you a handbook of NDA."

He was delighted to meet me I saw a spark in his eyes. He invited me to join NCC. He called me in the college library after college. It was two o'clock & we both hadn't eaten yet. We started our journey in the morning at 6 o'clock and up to 8 o'clock we were in the college. We crossed 12 k.m. within two hours. He took out my background & short biography. He advised me to attend the college every day. The college was over at 1:00 p.m.. But he instructed the librarian to keep watch on us. He also wanted us to study in the library after classes up to 5:00 p.m.But he allowed us to go early because it was our first day. We came out of the college. There was a canteen on the college premises. But that was not our area. The others gathered there and we started our marching and stopped at Hanuman Mandir, My Naru's favourite temple, we sat under it and opened a white Shabby knotted cloth with Bhakri and garlic chutney. We devoured eat. We reached home in the evening. Mangala Tai watched us from a long distance. I told Mai and Grandmother about what had happened.

Grandmother roared, 'I won't allow you to enter the Fauj, you know people are dying in Fauj and you want to go there, you are our last hope, we people are very much happy in our state, why do you want to leave us, you can become a police, doctor, teacher or come with me to taluka, I will give you a job under Marwadi for hisab Kitab. You can gain handsome money".

Naru smartly answer Grandma, "Ajji, to enter in Fauj means not a soldier, Have you remembered any British officer, Janya will act or live like that, he will have a car and bungalow, and he will send other men for firing".

"Accha is it right Jana?" Ajji asked.

"Yes," I said.

" But whenever you become, promise me, not to send soldiers for firing to the enemy. It is a great sin to push people in trouble after, they have their families, promise me",Grandmother looked at me with hope.

" Ok, I won't send them to war or fight with enemies," I satisfied her curiosity. We started our journey in the early morning the next day, On half of the road Maruti 800 car stopped beside us. A girl who wore black specs invited us to board in car. She was prime attraction of our class. Everyone wanted to make friendship with her.

She was fair,grandiose and the most beautiful girl of our class...... But I said sorry to her.

She repeated, "You can sit, don't be nervous. I am in your class. Yesterday I was very impressed by your attitude.

"But we don't need anyone's sympathy, it is okay that you are impressed by our attitude. but forgive us, we don't mind walking, it is good for our health. It makes us sturdy. I request you, don't paralyse, you can go, "I responded.

Naru shooked me, " Why not? We have to go, I didn't sit in a car".

I stopped him & said, "If you wish to board you can go, don't force me."

Naru understood my attitude & said thanks to her. She went fast. We reached on time into college. I fully concentrated on my studies. That car girl looked at me sometimes. I didn't ask her name on the way. After finishing our classes, all went to the canteen & we two went to the Botanical Garden for lunch. We left college at 5:00 p.m.. after study. Naru was weak in learning but slowly he had developed his taste in study. On our way home, that car girl slowed down her car, she matched up her speed with us for up to five minutes then took full speed. She spent her time in the canteen. She repeated the act every day but we did not respond. Soon, we entered the NCC Enrollment. On the day of Enrollment, one of the Army soldiers came, and he took our physical and oral exams. ANO Aher sir gave both of us first preference. We received a Khaki uniform, shoes & batches. We dedicatedly served in the NCC. The NCC parade, drill, and activities taught us unity and discipline. NCC is India's second line of Defence. Mostly, I learned time management at NCC. I received special favours from Aher sir. He selected both of us for the SSB coaching camp. I was highly surprised that Naru was selected with me. I thought Naru was lagging in study and communication. But he was confidently speaking English without hesitation though he made grammatical mistakes but Finally he was with me, my best & only friend.

If he was not with me, I might have left education because I would have lost my father who showed me this universe & lovely sister who groomed me. Sometimes, I thought, I had to end my life but I remember my Appa's words, " Jana, you don't care whether I would with you or not but you have to crack our destiny our, fortunes. Those are believe in good fortune tell them we can make our destiny, our fortunes, our fates. Those are believe in good fortunes, tell them we can make our destiny with our efforts. We are own creators of our fortunes. One more thing, you are the lighthouse for our people, our community, our confraternity ".

Appa's words did not sink me into the negative thoughts. They dragged me from the nostalgia. After leaving the universe, Appa was continuously with me, he was moving around me like a nymph. He advised me, and he helped me in my decision & I thought his soul remained with me because I did not complete the dream and fulfil the desire of Appa.

We were both selected in the NCC camp at Pune in the next month. so, we went to the National Defence Academy Khadakwasla, Pune. The surrounding and British architecture of NDA haunted us. It was only a day camp. We woke early at 4 a.m. We prepared ourselves within 10 minutes & went for the ground activities, lectures & sports in the evening & oral interview at night. On the last day, we both returned with a rich packet of experience from the camp. We reached home exhausted. As soon as we reached home in the evening, we heard the roaring sound of the Maruti car. The car girl came home.

She called from the door" Has Jana come?"

Soon, my Grandmother came, she held her hand & said," You must come in, they have reached before some hours, who are you? What is your name? You have been enquiring to him since last week".

"I am Meena Balu Patil, I am studying with him, I came here to take notes from him.....", She hesitated.

"Balu Patil, "Are you his daughter....?" Grandmother raised her eyebrows. “You are my special guest now, you must come in, Bala Patil is our inspirational spirit...!".

Grandma introduced her to all of us & she warned me to help Meena in all her ways in fact, she commanded me to go with her & gave company to her. I did not want to argue with Grandma. I gave her my notes, she smiled & went away.

Grandma congratulated me for winning her enticement. But I told her that nobody would distract me from my aim. She responded, "You don't know anything about her father, Her father spoiled my doll's life, he suppressed my Dattu's life, he seduced my lovely granddaughter and since I did not believe in God!Now, God has justice. He gives us an equal chance to take revenge. Insaans bad burning karmas reappeared to him like Boomerang. My heart will soothe after you engage with her or you can do the same with her, This is the best option, It will give her a stigma or you must spoil her chastity. Whatever you can do but don't leave her, you have full support...............".

I saw the burning revenge in her eyes and talk.

"Stop Attya, please stop, If we behave like them, act like them, then there would be no difference remaining between them and us, You must know, that your son did not like to take revenge, he didn't misuse his power, he took revenge against Bala Patil at starting. But he said we are peaceful people and children of Nature. Jana, you must focus on your goal rather than her. Your first goal is to fulfil your Appa's dream. You must become a government servant. And you are not only our last hope but also our confraternity. You have to show a way of progress to all of us. Remember, you will gain only one thing in life, if you fall in love, that will give you trouble and drag you from your family, your dream & your career. If you are living away from that you can drag your family from the muds of poverty, hard work, and begging. You can help our society & children to set their careers in various fields. But you must keep in mind that attraction towards the opposite sex is the sweetest thing in our world, even if it is sweeter than honey. It is not easy to come out from the hallucination of love & attraction. I will permit you to fall in love but this is not the right time, the right age. Your age is an age of walking on the fire. Now, you decide to take which side, you would sink us in the same condition or leave us on the apex of the settlement", My mother wittily advised me.

Destiny helped me to make mature decisions. My destiny was nothing but my Appa. Who showed me the way in any conflict. I soothed my Grandma and my mother. I promise them that I will fulfil my Appa's dream. My Grandmother muttered something, she clenched her fist and went away from home. I indemnified her that I wouldn't lose track.

CHAPTER FIFTEEN

Twist

The Next day, we were in college and busy completing the remaining study, deeply engrossed in revising the topics & forgot about our return. We left college at 7:30 p.m. It was a dark night in September. We both started marching towards home. Suddenly, a Maruti 800 car stopped beside us. Naru forced me to get in & I was exhausted & not able to walk for a long time. So, I boarded in a car, that was our first time to board in the private car. She invited me to sit in front of her. Naru was in the back seat. After a few minutes we crossed 10 km. & she stopped the car on the road where there were no signs of habitats, no power light, and only night accompanied us. The car's light did not allow darkness to come near us. She off the front lights, and only a micro bulb's blue light visualised our faces but not clear.

She came very close to me, "You didn't ask my name yet, dear?"

Naru insisted us, "I think we must go & should not stay here, why do we stop here?".

"Naru you don't have manners that if two young birds are talking, not to disturb them. We are talking and looking at each other, you don't have the right to disturb us, Please close your eyes and ears, don't look at us & disturb us. You must become a scarecrow," Meena fired on Naru.

She looked at me with a lecherous look. She clenched my right hand and moved towards me, "I am deeply mad at you, Jana, You haunted me".

Her lips were very much near to my lips. She touched her rosy petals lips on my lips & started kissing but I pushed her & kept my hand on her lips.

"You are wrong my dear, I don't want to be involved in you", I neglected her.

"Why not? don't think, I am from the upper class and you are from the Adivasis strata. I want you and that is final, I am a daughter of Patil & I will do according to my desire", she answered me.

"You and me, we both are two banks of a river, which can't be united, you are an angel and me a working beggar. My vision is clear and I can't give you a place in my vision", I asserted.

"Whatever your vision I love you madly, I don't know the connection, my mind is attracted towards you. We were indulged in our past birth. The whole night I was thinking of you. When you left for the camp I did not go to college only came to your Basti & returned. I was counting the days, the biggest days. I am very sorry but I am mad at you. I am following you. I can't live in this world or rebel against anyone for you. I can't compare you with anyone, you are the Masterpiece, my lord. Please accept me, I will serve you like a serf", She begged.

I took a long breath, still, she didn't flick her eyes off me. She steered at me continuously.

I smiled, "Do you really love me?

"Yes, I am", She replied.

So, "Can you follow my advice," I asked.

"Why not? I am under your patronage," She answered.

"Listen, Meena, My first love is my goal, my dream. For it, I sacrificed many things, even to fulfil my desire, my Appa sacrificed his life, and I have lost my dear sisters. My Appa handed over the responsibility of my confraternity on my shoulder. I will involve with you only after fulfil my desire. I want to become an Army officer. This dream haunted me, it couldn't make me sleep. I can't live without it. I request you, "If you really love me, don't come on my way like a hurdle." After fulfilling my dream, I will come to propose to you. Still, you have to wait without disturbing my concentration on my study. You must know if a youngster wants to come out of poor strata, he has to face many obstacles even if he has to fight with his destiny, Nature and God's will. Sometimes, he has to lose all his nearest and dearest, that time if you believe in him, he will reach the apex of his goal. My aim is to crack the NDA exam in my first attempt. And to reach my goal, you must help me, you become my booster, you can help me only by staying away from me. I promise you, I will return to you still then allow me to focus on my target," I assured her.

"It is impossible to stay away from you but the first time you demanded something from me & I gave you my assurance because I really love you," she smiled.

"Love means not to come together & live, the most important side of love is sacrifice, Radha Mata Ji allowed Krishna to live Mathura for doing his Karma. Love means worship, Pooja. Love means not to leave our lover in trouble. Love is understanding, adjustment & compromise with faith." I soothed her dilemma, and curiosity & took relief with a sigh.

She did not fully agree with me but her understanding of the situation was temporal. She left us near our home & left.

"My God! What to terrible disaster, She was! If I were in your place, I would dive into the sea of her love, what a scene, how you control yourself when a piece of sweet mithai is on your lips," Naru teased me. I looked at him angrily & he stopped his talk.

I spent more and more time in the library & managed my schedule but never got in her car. That was my first and last ride with her. She steered me every day in the classroom. But I showed her that I didn't notice her. The year passed & I got 95% in the result. But the calamities became my family members, how could I forget? My destiny was not to allow my life to go smoothly on the track of life.

On a certain day, Naru's uncle reached home in a car. He entered at home and looked at Naru. Naru understood something and started packaging his luggage.

Uncle asked, "Don't you tell Mangal to pack?".

Naru negatively said, "No, she should stay here, this is her family now, don't force her".

I did not understand what happened. Before I asked Naru, mother scolded Naru, "What happened Naru, Why are you starting packaging?." He didn't answer and took out his clothes, and books.

Mai shaked him, "Did anyone scold you ? You are calling me Mai, your mother & you hid something from me."

I grabbed his shirt's collar, "You are not revealing the truth, I am your brother dear, what's wrong with you?"....... I urged him.

"Listen, Mai, Jana, Mangal Tai, Ajji, When Appa passed away, One day my uncle came to meet me. My uncle & aunty don't have their children. He wanted to adopt me. That's why, he legally transferred the land in my name. But he didn't dare to come before my father's detention. Uncle offered me that he would bear the whole expenditures of my family and your study on a condition. I accepted the pact but I requested him to allow me for a year to live with you at least I would prepare my mind to stay away from you. I am very well known that you all try to break the pacts with uncle but I promised him to live with them except Mangal Tai. Sometimes we have to think professionally. Right now to fulfil our desires & dreams, we need money & together we can't gain. Love, affection, and emotions can push our lives but can't lift us from the present situation. We must try to accept our negative mind's decision. I persuaded my mind like a mature person", Naru advised us.

"But Naru you kept a secret from us, It heartens my heart," I asserted to him.

"Dost, separation cannot break our relations. Remember you tried to convince Meena on a certain day like me. I am trying to convince you. Love can't feed us, grow us, or help us to reach our goals. Just imagine if Soni Tai would be with us. She would live away from us to earn & send her earnings to all of us. So, I am like her, going to serve & earn somewhere. I promise I will come on every special occasion," he answered and touched the feet of Mai, Grandma &Mangal Tai.

Mai and Mangal Tai hugged him. "I request you Tai, take care of Mai and Grandma and help my brother in his study," Naru added.

Mai started crying and yelling.

"Don't cry Mai if you all showing distress, I can't move my foot," he silently spoke.

He addressed me, "Remember, I am leaving you, only because of you, I compromised with my destiny only for your sake. If you call me brother, promise me to attain my desire & my desire is "Don't show me your face until you become an officer. I sold & Sacrifice myself only for yourself dear," .

"I owe you, I met you after reaching to my goal & tested Boronia's success," I assured him.

Before Naru decided to leave I thought Naru didn't have a command in sudden difficulty & he was a preposterous person. But he became an erudite person. How could I forget he had lost his parents before me? & that incident stuck with him.

" One more thing, you all do not need to go to work. I will be sending money from time to time", he added & lifted his bags & luggage.

I snatched his luggage & held him & kept him in the uncle's car. His uncle was a politician & wealthy man. He was in search of his heir. Uncle wanted to groom Naru's attire as a politician. I understood Naru's intention. He wanted to climb the ladder of success by taking the hands of his uncle. Naru was not selfish but he knew without his uncle's support he could not help me & my family. I convinced my mind. From the moment he became Idol for me. He was the pathfinder of my career. I entered in 11th class & my fees were paid by Naru's uncle also set of NDA exam & Navneet for the 12th study. He offered me a bicycle to travel but I refused, I accepted study materials as a loan but my brother convinced me not to think like. I persuaded my mind that I had mortgaged my brother there. Every day, I used to walk towards college, and that walk kept me fit, During travelling I recapitulated the learned things in my class. That was my meditation. My recapitalisation means remembering the studied things in class on the way to home. Naru visited on the occasion of Raksha Bandhan, this time I was really surprised to see him. He had changed himself. He wore a pair of blue rough & tough jeans, a black Re-ban spectacle. He embraced me. The sweet boronia of Attar covered my clumsy, shattered home surroundings. His cleaned, iron-white shirts sparkled at my home. He had four Golden ring fingers in his left hand. The golden bracelet on his right hand showed that he had become a wealthy sheth. He brought three Yeola Paithanies to Mai, Ajji & Mangal Tai. My Juggi became a settlement of ladies' angels. My three ladies were shining in my home.

I asked him, "You told me not to show my face before reaching my goal and you are here, you broke your words".

He smartly answered me, "I told you not to show your face but that means not I don't want to see your face, I am here to see you & show you that I get my path & now this is your turn. I fixed my target to enter politics & don't want to miss this chance. You know God is giving each & every person a chance to change his or her destiny, those who take the first chance given by God, will reach the apex of success. I am with you brother but prove yourself. Now I am moving, my time is over. Uncle filled nomination for MLA election. I won't get time to meet you all." Naru touched the feet of all & hugged me.

He boarded into a White Ambassador and went. Mangal Tai nervously said to Mai, "Mai, What do you think about Naru, he has completely changed, I think he will definitely forgive us after time crossing, he won't like to come here again."

Mai confidently said, "No, your perception is wrong, he knew that he could not uplift us without his uncle's support, we must give respect to his sacrifice, he made the rash decision only for ourselves." That day Mai and Mangal Tai made a delicious feast with basundi. But the food became tasteless without the company of Naru.

The season for the final exam came. I entered the HSC board exam room. I found Meena seated exactly in the next row. I was peeping towards her. She was busy writing without sneaking me. She didn't peep out towards me nor look. She behaved like an intruder. I comforted my heart that she did not want to disturb my attention. The first English subject paper was over. Meena neither followed me nor came late behind me. When I came out of the class & marched towards my way, I thought she would offer me a lift to save my time but she had passed quickly in a car. I was surprised how a girl who had been mad at my love neglected me like a stranger.

I consoled my soul, "It is okay, she did it only for me".

But I didn't dare to talk with her. Our all students wanted to talk with her and make friends with her but since the first day, she has been in search of opportunities to meet with me. Now my heart impress was running towards her & she escaped. I gave all the papers with confidence. My paper was over & I appeared for the NDA exam. I started my study in deep. The exam was declared on the first Sunday of May. I choose 'Pune' as an exam centre. I had a month in my hand. I was mad at studying from down to Midnight. I had been studying History, Geography, General Knowledge, solving English Grammar and maths and taking notes in my notebooks.

On 26 April, I asked for money from Mai for my journey to Pune. She gave me a tattered five rupees note & said," This one is only one remaining & these are sunny days of Summer we can't gain money".

"But Naru sent money in the last month, Have you lost or spent?", I questioned.

Mai answered "I did not lose money but I spent on your Ajji's health. She has been suffering from some Gynaecological problem, since last month, if I didn't treat her, we might lose her. Now either you go to Naru or borrow money from somebody."

Suddenly, I walked towards Aher sir's home. I reached his home in the evening. He wore an undergarment and half pants. He was busy making supper. His wife was lying on the bed. His two children were busy in the study. I called him from the door, "Sir, Are you in ?"

"Who is there?", He asked.

"I am Jana, want to meet you",I replied.

"OK come in the kitchen", he permitted me.

I removed my slipper & went in. He was making roti.

Smiling on his face, He asked, "What do you want Janardan?" Why are you here?"

"Sir, I need your help", I said.

" Help! What can I do for you? He took Belan in his hand and stopped making roti," He questioned.

“I need money for my journey on my credit," I answered.

“The money! he laughed at me and said, "Do you think, I have a handsome salary. Then your perception is wrong. I can’t give you dear. I have my problems and I am finding solutions. I request you to find the solutions somewhere or start your journey by marching. I didn’t have enough salary like other teachers. I am helpless and treating my ill wife. I can’t explain more, if you don’t want to lose your faith, find out innovative solutions, I can give you only my luck." He comforted me and I left.

I reached home late in the night. I started my packaging. Mai asked, "Have you received money from anyone to go?

I smiled and said "Yes, I got money from my teacher for my voyage. I will start my journey in the morning."

"Why are you going too early to Pune, Baji? Mangal Tai asked.

" I want to match up with the environment of Pune", I satisfied her.

Soon, someone knocked on the door and it was Meena. She entered the home. I was shocked to see her in a saree. She had applied red Kumkum on her forehead and hair. She wore mangalsutra. "Meena, you are here why?", I questioned her.

She replied, "Jana, I got married and I came here to give you money. I went to Taluka with my groom for shopping and met Aher sir there. He told me about you. This is your money."

"But how are you married? What happened to you?", I trembled.

She continued, "It was a remarkable journey with you. I wanted to spend my life with you. Before our final exam, my father had a heart attack and he became paralyzed. He lay on the bed and counting his last days. He was worried about me in his last days. His final desire was to see my marriage. He opened his last wish in front of me, I was not ready for him, he knew I was mad in love. Even my all family members knew. My grandmother fixed my marriage with the son of the sarpanch of the near village. They arranged my marriage within a week. It was fixed last Sunday. I decided to elope but the day before my marriage my father died in front of me. Before his death, I gave my assurance to him and I married the boy. Now he is waiting for me outside the home. I beg you, if you respect my love accept my help and go for the exam. I would like to see you in uniform. Lastly, forgive me, if you can. I won't come to your way again good my dear." She stood up quickly wiped out her tears. She haned over five hunded repees note and ran away.

I was stunned for an hour and didn't move from my place. This was another slap of my destiny. I could not understand which shocks I had to bear in my life. My mother took me in her lap at night. I was deeply thinking about Meena. I fell in love with her. I saw and felt her existence everywhere. She was with me, I thought I had become mad in her love. She appeared in front of me, she took shelter in my heart. It is really difficult to uproot our first love, from the heart. I was unable to forgive her. Her aura did not let me leave. I could not sleep in the night.

Appa came near me after midnight. “Are you in love Jana?”, He asked.

"Yes, I am and I can’t forgive her, I didn’t remember her before, but today, her aura haunted me and I felt sorry for her. If I accepted her proposal, I would live with her peacefully, Appa", I replied.

“Humm! You must know, Lord Shri Krishna could not marry Radha Rani, intentionally. One day Radha Rani, asked Sri Krishna "Why did you not marry me, dear?" Lord Shri Krishna replied "You and me are one, our soul is one, we and our soul are not separated, so how could I marry with you? If we are one”. The same theory applies to all lovers and beloveds. We humans are generally haunted by either love and affection or deeds. If love and affection rule over one’s mind, one can’t walk on the path of success and if one walks on the path of deeds he might fail to win love. Some rare persons succeed in gaining both, "Appa soothed my mind.

"But how can I overcome her nostalgia?", I asked.

"If I say don’t think of her, your mind would continuously think about her, So I would like to suggest you, ask your mind, why should I think about her? Life becomes meaningless or it has meaning without her. Whether the family members and present family situation has changed or not? What differences you can find when she leaves your life? Or if you reached your goal or not? Or if you reach success or a goal without her and you would marry another girl, how your life would be affected? Search for the answers and find quick solutions or simply think, we cannot stop time. And think...Currently, I am focusing on my exam after finishing the exam I will have my remaining life to take action to think about what had happened to me. Still calm the negative side of your brain, just focus on your exam because NDA is India's one of the toughest exams and around lacs of students appear to it every year. Best luck dear. Meena will be happy to see you in uniform. After reaching your goal many Meenas will follow you. She has sacrificed her life because her parents grew her, they fulfilled her all desires and it was her ought to follow the words and advices of her parents like a good daughter. So don't think that daughters and sons have to revolt against their dearest parents only for a few days love. You must control your teenager's mind," Appa disappeared after persecution.

CHAPTER SIXTEEN

The Final Move

I changed my perception, soon I woke up, the saffron rays of the Sun occupied the mountains of the East. Small sparrows and bulbuls were chirping. A loud yell of cock jiggles our confraternity. The soft voice of the Hanuman temple bell bestirs my spirit to move towards my goal. The next day, I had to appear for an exam. I packed a nylon carry bag. I saw Ashirwad from my three iron women. My grandmother kissed my forehead. This time, her eyes looked tiresome, and she hugged me. Her hands did not remain strong enough to bear my load of body. I touched her feet and moved. After walking for two hours, I reached Taluka and took a bus to Nashik City or the city of pilgrims. I got off at the Nashik bus stand in the evening. I had attended NCC camp with her NCC instructor via the same route. So I did not face any difficulty in the journey. I arrived at Nashik railway station and marched towards the ticket counter. I asked for a ticket from the counter, he demanded 20 Rupees. I took my hand in my pocket and I found my pocket was torn. I lost my money. I was perplexed and shrugged off from the line of tickets. I sat down restlessly in a corner. One of the sages sat beside me. He wanted to go to Kashi a holy City.

He inquired me, "I think you don't have money to travel but I can help you".

I asked him instantly, "How can you help me?"

"Just board on train in the general compartment and sit near the toilet but remember while get off you must leave the station as soon as possible and don't come under the surveillance of the ticket checker," He guided me.

I boarded a train and started my journey, I sat near the toilet. The dirty odour of the surroundings started my headache. I arrived at Pune in the early morning. The other persons from other states got off with me. Their clothes were shattered and clumsy like serfs. I mingled in that crowd. The crowd came near the entrance gate & caught by the ticket checker. The ticket checker called the police and he handed over us all to the police. The policeman came & the passengers without tickets boarded in van one by one. I felt suffocated & urged the policeman that I didn't want to travel but I had to take my exam. Fortunately, I kept the hall ticket in my carry bag. I took out the hall ticket & showed him. He stunned me & took me to his officer. I saluted the officer & explained what had happened. The officer said, "Don't worry dear, if you have a hall ticket for the exam, you are allowed to travel for the exam. By the way, from where do you have to belong?"

" Sir, I am from Devgrah a part of the Satmala region, an Adivasi area & want to become an officer in the Army", I answered.

He was impressed & looked kindly at my hall ticket. He said, "Only two hours remaining for the exam & you have to present there an hour before the exam, you looked tense & hungry, the exam centre is far away from it, how can you manage?

" I will run, I am a good runner but please relieve me", I begged him.

" It's okay but don't run, My men will leave you there," He said & called to the policeman. "Leave him urgently to the exam centre, in my jeep", He ordered.

I sat in the police Jeep & they left me at the exam spot before the exam started. I paid gratitude to the policeman & touched their feet. I used my ability to take exams. I attended seventy-eight per cent questions for the remaining questions I was not sure about. I came out of the hall after attempting. I was satisfied with my performance.

Now, I questioned myself," How can I go home?

At the time I heard a familiar voice, I was shocked to see Naru there. He was in a white tidy uniform with his spects. I relived a sigh of tension.

He said, "Thank God, I found you. I am sorry, I could not arrive on time to pick up you at home. I reached late there. I inquired about your exam centre to Mangal Tai, she told me everything. I was ashamed that I failed to leave you before your exam in my Ambassador. I was busy in propaganda for my uncle's election. But don't worry, we will go in our car. Let's move, first, we eat somewhere & go."

I didn't reply to him only smiling because I was eager to listen to his continuous talk. He was talking continuously without stopping throughout the whole journey. He promised to come with me at the time of the Service Selection Board and also warned me, not to seek help from anyone. He dropped at home but without meeting anyone he hurriedly went. I received the result after thirty days via post. The same postman immediately informed my news to Naru. Naru came home a day before my SSB interview. He bought new black leather shoes, socks a belt, a white shirt, black pants, a tie, a white handkerchief a Parker pen. I did not have any idea to wear shoes. So, Naru had already hired a person who was well-reversed in grooming. He taught me how to wear a tie, wear shoes & how to walk. My mother was delighted to see me in that attire. Soon, we move towards Khadkwasala, Pune in the NDA training centre.

The gatekeeper didn't allow anyone to enter the centre except the candidate. Naru assured me that he would wait outside the gate. I observed the other candidates wore neat clothes. They were following manners. They all looked like officers except me. My body spread a light odour of sweat. The other candidates spread sweet smells of talcum powder as well as perfumes. I was a little ashamed & walked slowly at last behind them. One of the newly recruited instructors showed us a way towards the reception hall. All moved fast. When I walked the all lights & fans in the corridor were running. I switched off unnecessary articles. The reception welcomed us & gave us as scheduled. The schedule began the next day. We were allotted homes for living, a duo lived in a room. The instructor told us to choose a buddy for yourself. No one was interested in choosing me as their buddy. Most of them were sons of officers from the North India region. Only three candidates were from South India state. One candidate was from Tamil Nadu. Murugan accepted me as his buddy. His mother was a Marathi lady, so he knew the Marathi language very well. But he was weak in Hindi & fluent in English. His grandfather was Nayab Subedar in the Indian Army. So, he knew the procedure of SSB & I had already learnt the procedure in the NCC SSB camp. I remembered the camp & techniques trend by our Colonel. The next day was the day of group discussion & description of a picture. The topic was whether computer replaces the working ability of humans. I & Murugan laid positive sides of arguments. The next phase was picture composition & there was a picture of a lady who carried a bucket on her head and marched towards the village. That picture was not new for me. Most of us answered the picture was related to drought & the village did not have water resources except well outside the habitat.

But I answered, "She is a woman from a backward class & to calm the thirst of her family members. She is fetching water from a well, which is from the backward class. And she looks so happy that she got water for her family, maybe her husband went to work & she has children, so nobody with her to help. Because she thinks to carry children near well is dangerous".

My answer impressed the members of the board & they selected me for the next round. When we entered we were seven hundred candidates now, we remained four hundred. I supported Murgan & he was with me for the next round. The next day, we faced a physical exam & obstacles. I easily climbed on the rope & crawled on the monkey rope. I quickly crossed all hurdles & barriers & gained the top position in running. That time I realised, destiny had been taking my practice since childhood & made me a skillful person in crossing the hurdles easily. The final day was the day of the interview & we were two hundred candidates.

The interview begins sharply at 9:00 a.m. as per schedule. My number was Nineteen. I neatly practised to wear clothes, tie & black shoes. My hair was already cut before coming to SSB. Whenever the candidate came out of the facing interview everyone was curious to ask the interviewer about his performance. Soon, Appa sat near me & suggested I keep quiet. I did not dare to ask anyone how was the interview. Soon the doorkeeper called my chest number to come into the interview hall. My heart was beating fast, my legs were shivering, and the cold sweat came out from my forehead. But Appa patted me & told me to take a long breath & controlled my breath. I followed his advice. Soon, my leg stopped shivering & my heart turned into a normal situation. Within a minute, I was in front of the interviewers. The Brigadier was head of the panel & four colonels, and two Lieutenant colonels were there. They asked me for my introduction. I fluently introduced myself & explained my academic performance since my eighth standard. One by one they started their questions. I remembered following a few of them.

Q.: In which field you would like to serve NDA?

Ans: I would like to serve in Indian Army.

Q.: Why did you choose the Indian Army rather than the Navy or Air Force?

Ans.: My qualification matched with the Army only & I desire to enter the Indian Army that's why, I took the Arts stream.

Q.: Why did you choose NDA for your career?

Ans.: Sir, it is India's one of the toughest exams. It is a challenge for younger aspirants. I would like to accept the challenges. Apart from that, it is a highly reputed uniform service. To become part of the Indian Army is a matter of pride.

Q.: In which position you like to see yourself in the future?

Ans.: I would like to become a part of an inspirational history to others. People from my region are unaware of the entry of the Armed forces. I would like to become a part and parcel of the path for them. I will see myself in the highest position in the Army in future.

I answered all the questions asked by them. But I don't remember all the questions.

Finally, the Brigadier asked me " Is anyone from your family who served in the Armed forces?

I answered him, "No, but I added my great-grandfather & my great-great-grandfather took part in India's freedom fighting. Though they were not so much famous they loved their land, region & their men."

The process was over & I was doubted about my performance in the interview. I moved towards Naru's destination after saying goodbye to Murugan. But Naru was confident about my performance. We reached home the next day in Naru's Ambassador. When we entered our home, we found my grandma lying on the floor, She was moaning, and I held her hand tightly.

Naru suggested, "We will move her into the hospital, let's go."

But she stopped us & said, "Please, I don't want to go to the hospital, I want to die here. The doctor has diagnosed me with cancer & it is in the last stage. I have been counting the days since we went to the hospital, We three knew about my illness. But we kept it secret from ourselves. Please don't force me to come to the hospital. It is my last wish. We have to leave everyone on a certain day. If you drag me to the hospital, my soul would roam here only, I would not gain Moksha".

She touched my cheeks & held my nose. A loud sound hitched come outside her mouth & she remained calm & wordless. Her eyes & mouth remained open. Her hand came down quickly while touching me. She died. We did her cremation but this time rain did not appear. The burning fire of her body burnt my bad fortune on that day. On the tenth day of her death, I & Naru shaved our heads & did an auspicious performance.

We returned home & a postman greeted me. He said," Your Ajji blessed you with it."

He delivered a letter to me that was an appointment letter from the Indian Army. I was selected by the National Defence Academy, Pune as a Lieutenant. The postman gave me my dream. The tears poured from my eyes & hugged Naru. After a few years, I married SSC passed girl from my community and educated her to her post-graduation. Naru became MLA & married the wealthy daughter of a politician. We arranged Mangal Tai's marriage with a teacher. Now, I have two children & I am an Officer in the Indian Army, my wife is running an Academy of Armed Forces for tribal students in our region. Naru is a tribal Minister of Maharashtra & seeking his highest position but he did not have any child like his uncle. Chanda Tai is normal & she has a girl. My Mai, mother is living with Naru. Naru doesn't let her leave his home. One more thing, I did not meet Appa after joining NDA & I had been trying to meet him but he never came. So, I learnt from my destiny, "If a tree can't bend in a windy rain, it will be uprooted by the force, and we should not wait for our fortune but we have to create our fortune."

Jai Hind.!

www.ingramcontent.com/pod-product-compliance
Lightning Source LLC
LaVergne TN
LVHW090051160826
845672LV00015B/1640

* 9 7 9 8 8 9 1 3 3 6 5 4 4 *